The Dutch Cheese

books by Walter de la Mare

★

The Magic Jacket and Other Stories
The Old Lion and Other Stories
The Scarecrow and Other Stories
Stories from the Bible
The Three Royal Monkeys
Animal Stories
Early One Morning
Behold this Dreamer
Desert Islands
Memoirs of a Midget
The Return
On the Edge and Other Stories
The Riddle and Other Stories

WALTER DE LA MARE

THE DUTCH CHEESE

AND OTHER STORIES

illustrated by Irene Hawkins

FABER AND FABER LIMITED
24 Russell Square
London

First published this edition in Mcmxlvi
by Faber and Faber Limited
24 Russell Square London W.C.1
Printed in Great Britain by
Purnell and Sons Limited
Paulton (Somerset) and London

Contents

The Dutch Cheese

Once—once upon a time there lived, with his sister Griselda, in a little cottage near the Great Forest, a young farmer whose name was John. Brother and sister, they lived alone, except for their sheep-dog, Sly, their flock of sheep, the numberless birds of the forest, and the fairies. John loved his sister beyond telling; he loved Sly; and he delighted to listen to the birds singing at twilight round the darkening margin of the forest. But he feared and hated the fairies. And, having a very stubborn heart, the more he feared, the more he hated them; and the more he hated them, the more they pestered him.

Now these were a tribe of fairies, sly, small, gay-hearted and mischievous, and not of the race of fairies noble, silent, beautiful and remote from man. They were a sort of gipsy fairies, very nimble and of aery and prankish company, and partly for mischief and partly for love of her they were always trying to charm John's dear sister Griselda away, with their music and fruits and trickery. He more than half believed it was they who years ago had decoyed into the forest not only his poor old father, who had gone out faggot-cutting in his sheepskin hat with his ass; but his mother too, who soon after, had gone out to look for him.

But fairies, even of this small tribe, hate no man. They mocked him and mischiefed him; they spilt his milk, rode astraddle on his rams, garlanded his old ewes with sow-thistle and briony, sprinkled water on his kindling wood, loosed his bucket into the well, and hid his great leather shoes. But all this they did, not for hate—for they came and went like evening moths about Griselda—but because in his fear and fury he shut up his sister from them, and because he was sullen and stupid. Yet he did nothing but fret himself. He set

traps for them, and caught starlings; he fired his blunderbuss at them under the moon, and scared his sheep; he set dishes of sour milk in their way, and sticky leaves and brambles where their rings were green in the meadows; but all to no purpose. When at dusk, too, he heard their faint, elfin music, he would sit in the door blowing into his father's great bassoon till the black forest re-echoed with its sad, solemn, wooden voice.

But that was of no help either. At last he grew so surly that he made Griselda utterly miserable. Her cheeks lost their scarlet and her eyes their sparkling. Then the fairies began to plague John in earnest—lest their lovely, loved child of man, Griselda, should die.

Now one summer's evening—and most nights are cold in the Great Forest—John, having put away his mournful bassoon and bolted the door, was squatting, moody and gloomy, with Griselda on his hearth beside the fire. And he leaned back his great hairy head and stared straight up the chimney to where high in the heavens glittered the Seven Sisters. And suddenly, while he lolled there on his stool watching this starry seven, there appeared against the dark sky a mischievous, elvish head secretly peeping down at him; and busy fingers began sprinkling dew on his wide upturned face. He heard the laughter too of the fairies miching and gambolling on his thatch, and in a rage he started up; seized a round Dutch cheese that lay on a platter, and with all his force threw it clean and straight up the sooty chimney at the faces of mockery clustered above. And after that, though Griselda sighed at her spinning wheel, he heard no more. Even the cricket that had been whistling all through the evening fell silent, and John supped on his black bread and onions alone.

Next day Griselda woke at dawn and put her head out of the little window beneath the thatch, and the day was white with mist.

"'Twill be another hot day," she said to herself, combing her beautiful hair.

But when John went down, so white and dense with mist were the fields, that even the green borders of the forest were invisible, and the whiteness went to the sky. Swathing and wreathing itself, opal and white as milk, all morning the mist grew thicker and thicker about the little house. When John went out about nine o'clock to peer about him, nothing was to be seen at all. He could hear his sheep bleating, the kettle singing, Griselda sweeping, but straight up above him hung only, like a small round fruit, a little cheese-red beamless sun —straight up above him, though the hands of the clock were not yet come to ten. He clenched his fists and stamped in sheer rage. But no-one answered him, no voice mocked him but his own. For when these idle, mischievous fairies have played a trick on an enemy they soon weary of it.

All day long that little sullen lantern burned above the mist, sometimes red, so that the white mist was dyed to amber, and sometimes milky pale. The trees dripped water from every leaf. Every flower asleep in the garden was neckleted with beads; and nothing but a drenched old forest crow visited the lonely cottage that afternoon to cry: "Kah, Kah, Kah!" and fly away. But Griselda knew her brother's mood too well to speak of it, or to complain. And she sang on gaily in the house, though she was more sorrowful than ever.

Next day John went out to tend his flocks. And wherever he went the red sun seemed to follow. When at last he found his sheep they were drenched with the clinging mist and were huddled together in dismay. And when they saw him it seemed that they cried out with one unanimous bleating voice:

"O ma-a-a-ster!"

And he stood counting them. And a little apart from the rest stood his old ram Soll, with a face as black as soot; and there, perched on his back, impish and sharp and scarlet, rode and tossed and sang just such another fairy as had mocked John from the chimney-top. A fire

seemed to break out in his body, and, picking up a handful of stones, he rushed at Soll through the flock. They scattered, bleating, out into the mist. And the fairy, all-acockahoop on the old ram's back, took its small ears between finger and thumb, and as fast as John ran, so fast jogged Soll, till all the young farmer's stones were thrown, and he found himself alone in a quagmire so sticky and befogged that it took him till afternoon to grope his way put. And only Griselda's singing over her broth-pot guided him at last home.

Next day he sought his sheep far and wide, but not one could he find. To and fro he wandered, shouting and calling and whistling to Sly, till heartsick and thirsty, they were both wearied out. Yet bleatings seemed to fill the air, and a faint, beautiful bell tolled on out of the mist; and John knew the fairies had hidden his sheep, and he hated them more than ever.

After that he went no more into the fields, brightly green beneath the enchanted mist. He sat and sulked, staring out of the door at the dim forests far away, glimmering faintly red beneath the small red sun. Griselda could not sing any more, she was too tired and hungry. And just before twilight she went out and gathered the last few pods of peas from the garden for their supper.

And while she was shelling them, John, within doors in the cottage, heard again the tiny timbrels and the distant horns, and the odd, clear, grasshopper voices calling and calling her, and he knew in his heart that, unless he relented and made friends with the fairies, Griselda would surely one day run away to them and leave him forlorn. He scratched his great head, and gnawed his broad thumb. They had taken his father, they had taken his mother, they might take his sister—but he *wouldn't* give in.

So he shouted, and Griselda in fear and trembling came in out of the garden with her basket and basin and sat down in the gloaming to finish shelling her peas.

And as the shadows thickened and the stars began to shine, the malevolent singing came nearer, and presently there was a groping and stirring in the thatch, a tapping at the window, and John knew the fairies had come—not alone, not one or two or three, but in their company and bands—to plague him, and to entice away Griselda. He shut his mouth and stopped up his ears with his fingers, but when, with great staring eyes, he saw them capering like bubbles in a glass, like flames along straw, on his very doorstep, he could contain himself no longer. He caught up Griselda's bowl and flung it—peas, water and all—full in the snickering faces of the Little Folk! There came a shrill, faint twitter of laughter, a scampering of feet, and then all again was utterly still.

Griselda tried in vain to keep back her tears. She put her arms round John's neck and hid her face in his sleeve.

"Let me go!" she said, "let me go, John, just a day and a night, and I'll come back to you. They are angry with us. But they love me; and if I sit on the hillside under the boughs of the trees beside the pool and listen to their music just a little while, they will make the sun shine again and drive back the flocks, and we shall be happy as ever. Look at poor Sly, John dear, he is hungrier even than I am." John heard only the mocking laughter and the tap-tapping and the rustling and crying of the fairies, and he wouldn't let his sister go.

And it began to be marvellously dark and still in the cottage. No stars moved across the casement, no water-drops glittered in the candleshine. John could hear only one low, faint, unceasing stir and rustling all around him. So utterly dark and still it was that even Sly woke from his hungry dreams and gazed up into his mistress's face and whined.

They went to bed; but still, all night long, while John lay tossing on his mattress, the rustling never ceased. The old kitchen clock ticked on and on, but there came no hint of dawn. All was pitch-black and now all was utterly silent. There wasn't a whisper, not a creak, not a sigh of air, not a footfall of mouse, not a flutter of moth, not a settling of dust to be heard at all. Only desolate silence. And John at last could endure his fears and suspicions no longer. He got out of bed and stared from his square casement. He could see nothing. He tried to thrust it open; it would not move. He went downstairs and unbarred the door and looked out. He saw, as it were, a deep, clear, green shade, from behind which the songs of the birds rose faint as in a dream.

And then he sighed like a grampus and sat down, and knew that the fairies had beaten him. Like Jack's beanstalk, in one night had grown up a dense wall of peas. He pushed and pulled and hacked with his axe, and kicked with his shoes, and buffeted with his blunderbuss. But it was all in vain. He sat down once more in his chair beside the hearth and covered his face with his hands. And at last Griselda, too, awoke, and came down with her candle. And she comforted her brother, and told him if he would do what she bade she would soon make all right again. And he promised her.

So with a scarf she bound tight his hands behind him; and with a rope she bound his feet together, so that he could neither run nor throw stones, peas or cheeses. She bound his eyes and ears and mouth with a napkin, so that he could neither see, hear, smell, nor cry out. And, that done, she pushed and pulled him like a great bundle, and at last rolled him out of sight into the chimney-corner against the wall. Then she took a small sharp pair of needlework scissors that her godmother had given her, and snipped and snipped, till at last there came a little hole in the thick green hedge of peas. And putting her mouth there she called softly through the little hole. And the fairies drew near the doorstep and nodded and nodded and listened.

And then and there Griselda made a bargain with them for the forgiveness of John—a lock of her golden hair; seven dishes of ewes' milk; three and thirty bunches of currants, red, white and black; a bag of thistledown; three handkerchiefs full of lambs' wool; nine jars of honey; a peppercorn of spice. All these (except the hair) John was to bring himself to their secret places as soon as he was able. Above all, the bargain between was that Griselda would sit one full hour each evening of summer on the hillside in the shadow and greenness that slope down from the great Forest towards the valley, where the fairies' mounds are, and where their tiny brindled cattle graze.

Her brother lay blind and deaf and dumb as a log of wood. She promised everything.

And then, instead of a rustling and a creeping, there came a rending and clattering and crashing. Instead of green shade, light of amber; then white. And as the thick hedge withered and shrank, and the merry and furious dancing sun scorched and scorched and scorched, there came, above the singing of the birds, the bleatings of sheep—and behold sooty Soll and hungry Sly met square upon the doorstep; and all John's sheep shone white as hoarfrost on his pastures; and every lamb was garlanded with pimpernel and eyebright; and the old fat ewes stood still, with saddles of moss; and their laughing riders sat and saw Griselda standing in the doorway in her beautiful yellow hair.

As for John, tied up like a sack in the chimney-corner, down came his cheese again crash upon his head, and, not being able to say anything, he said nothing.

Lucy

Once upon a time there were three sisters, the Misses MacKnackery—or, better still, the Miss MacKnackeries. They lived in a large, white, square house called Stoneyhouse; and their names were Euphemia, Tabitha, and Jean Elspeth. They were known over Scotland for miles and miles, from the Tay to the Grampians—from the Tay to the Grumpy Ones, as a cousin who did not like Euphemia and Tabitha used to say.

Stoneyhouse had been built by the Miss MacKnackeries's grandfather, Mr. Angus MacKnackery, who, from being a poor boy with scarcely a bawbee in his breeches pocket, had risen up to be a wealthy manufacturer of the best Scotch burlap, which is a kind of sacking. He made twine, too, for tying up parcels. He would have made almost anything to make money. But at last, when he was sixty-six, he felt he would like to be a gentleman living in the country with a large garden to walk about in, flowers in beds, cucumbers in frames, pigs in sties, and one or two cows for milk, cream, and butter.

So he sold his huge, smoky works and warehouse, and all the twine and burlap, hemp, jute, and whalebone still in it, for £80,000. With this £80,000 he built Stoneyhouse, purchased some fine furniture and some carriages and horses, and invested what was over.

Jean Elspeth, when she was learning sums, and when

she had come to Interest—having sometimes heard her father and mother speak of her grandfather and of his fortune, and how he had *invested* it—just to please her governess, Miss Gimp, thought she would make a sum of it. So she wrote down in her rather straggly figures in an exercise book:

£80,000 @ £4 per centum per annum
=£80,000 x 4÷100=£32,000.

It was the first really enjoyable sum she had ever done. And yet Miss Gimp was a little put about when Jean Elspeth showed it to her father. Still, Mr. MacKnackery, senior, had been a really rich man, and regretted that the gentleman who bought his factory could never afterwards make such fine burlap as himself, nor even such durable twine.

He lived to be eighty, and then he died, leaving his money to his son, Robert Duncan Donald David, Jean Elspeth's father. And when *he* died, his dear wife Euphemia Tabitha being dead too, he left all that was over of the £80,000 (for, alas and alas! he had lost a good part of it) to his three daughters: Euphemia, Tabitha, and Jean Elspeth.

When Jean Elspeth was old enough to breakfast with the family in the big dining-room with the four immense windows, she used to sit opposite the portraits of her grandfather, her father, and her mother. They hung in heavy handsome gilt frames on the wall opposite the windows. And while in her high chair she gobbled up her porridge—and gobbled it up quickly, not so much because she liked it as because she hated being put in the corner for not eating it—she would sit and look at them.

Her grandfather's was by far the largest of the three

portraits, and it hung in the very middle of the lofty wall, under the moulded ceiling. He was a stout and imposing man, with bushy whiskers and cold bright blue eyes. The thumb and first finger of his right hand held

a fine thick Albert watchchain, which the painter had painted so skilfully that you could see it was eighteen-carat gold at a single glance. So he hung: for ever boldly staring down on his own great dining-room and all that was in it—yet not appearing to enjoy it very much.

What was more, her grandfather always looked exactly as if he were on the point of taking out his watch to see the time; and Jean Elspeth had the odd notion that, if he ever did succeed in so doing, its hands would undoubtedly point to a quarter to twelve. But she could no more have told you why, than she could tell you why she used to count each spoonful of her porridge, or why she felt happier when the last spoonful was an odd number.

The portrait of her father was that of a man much less stout and imposing than her grandfather. He was dark, and smiling, and he had no whiskers. And Jean Elspeth had loved him dearly. Every morning when she had finished her breakfast (and if nobody was looking) she would give a tiny little secret wave of the spoon towards him, as if he might be pleased at seeing her empty plate.

On the other side of her grandfather's portrait hung a picture of her mother. And the odd thing about this picture was that, if you looked long enough, you could not help seeing—as if it were almost the ghost of Jean Elspeth—her very own small face, peeping out of the paint at you, just like a tiny little green marmoset out of a cage all to itself in the Zoo. Jean Elspeth had discovered this when she was only seven; but Euphemia and Tabitha had never noticed it at all.

They knew they were far less like their mother (who had been a Miss Reeks MacGillicuddy of Kelso) than their grandfather. Still they were exceedingly proud of *that*. As for Jean Elspeth, they didn't think she was like any of the family at all. Indeed, Euphemia had more than once remarked that Jean Elspeth had "nae deegnity", and Tabitha that "she micht jist as weel ha' been a changeling". Even now, when they were elderly ladies, they always treated her as if she were still not very far from being a child, though, after all, Jean Elspeth was only five years younger than Tabitha.

But then, how different she was in looks! For while Tabitha had a long pale face a little like a unicorn's, with mouse-coloured hair and green-grey eyes, Jean Elspeth was dark and small, with red in her cheek and a tip to her nose. And while Tabitha's face changed very little, Jean Elspeth's was like a dark little glancing pool on an April morning. Sometimes it looked almost centuries older than either of her sisters', and then, again, sometimes it looked simply no age at all.

It depended on what she was doing—whether she was sitting at seven o'clock dinner on Great Occasions, when the Bults, and the McGaskins, and Dr. Menzies were guests, or merely basking idly in the sunshine at her bedroom window. Jean Elspeth would sometimes, too, go wandering off by herself over the hills a mile or two away from the house. And *then* she looked not a minute older than looks a harebell, or a whinchat, perched with his white eyebrow on a fuzz-bush near a lichenous half-hidden rock among the heather.

However sad, too, she looked, she never looked grim. And even though (at dinner parties) she parted her hair straight down the middle, and smoothed the sides over as sleek as satin, she simply could not look what is called "superior". Besides, she had lips that were the colour of cherries, and curious quick hands that she was sometimes compelled to clasp together lest they should talk even more rapidly than her tongue.

Now in Stoneyhouse nobody—except perhaps the tweeny-maid and the scullery-maid, Sally and Nancy McGullie, who were cousins—ever talked *much*. It was difficult even to tell exactly how wise and sagacious and full of useful knowledge Euphemia and Tabitha were, simply because except at meals they so seldom opened their mouths. And never to sing.

This, perhaps, was because it is impossible to keep order if everybody's tongue keeps wagging. It wastes time, too; for only very few people can work hard and talk hard both at the same moment. And in Stoneyhouse everything was in apple-pie order (except the beds), and nobody ever wasted *any* time (except kissing time).

And yet, although time was never wasted, nobody seemed to be very much the better off for any that was actually "saved". Nobody had ever managed to pack some of it up in neat brown-paper parcels, or to put it in a bank as Mr. MacKnackery, senior, had put his money, or to pour it into jars like home-made jam. It just went. And in Stoneyhouse (until, at least, Euphemia one morning received a certain letter) it went very very slowly. The big hands of its clocks seemed to be envious of the little ones. They crept like shadows. And between their "tick" and their "tock" at times yawned a huge hole, as dark as a cellar. So, at least, Jean Elspeth fancied.

One glance at Stoneyhouse, even from the outside, would tell you how orderly it was. The four high white walls, with their large square slate roof fixed firmly on top of them, stood stiff as bombardiers on extremely solid foundations, and they on even solider rock. No tree dared cast a shadow upon them, no creeper crept. The glossy windows, with their straight lines of curtains behind them, just stared down on you as if they said, "Find the faintest speck or smear or flaw in us if you can!" And you hadn't the courage even to try.

It was just so inside. Everything was frozen in its

place. Not only the great solid pieces of furniture which Mr. MacKnackery had purchased with his burlap money—wardrobes, coffers, presses, four-posters, highboys, sideboards, tables, sofas, and oak chairs—but even all the little things, bead-mats, footstools, candle-snuffers, boot-trees, ornaments, knick-knacks, Euphemia's silks and Tabitha's water-colours. There was a place for everything, and everything was in its place. Yes, and it was kept there.

Except in Jean Elspeth's room. She had never never learned to be tidy, not even in her sums. She was constantly taking things out, and either forgetting to put them away again, or putting them away again in their wrong places. And do you suppose she blamed herself for this? Not at all. When she lost anything and had been looking for it for hours and hours—a book, or a brooch, or a ribbon, or a shoe—she would say to herself, laughing all over, "Well now, there! That *Lucy* must have hidden it!" And presently *there* it would be, right in the middle of her dressing-table or under a chair, as if a moment before it had been put back there; just for fun.

And who was this "*Lucy*"? There couldn't be a more difficult question; and Jean Elspeth had never attempted to answer it. It was one of those questions she never even asked herself. At least, not out loud. This, perhaps, was because she hated the thought of hurting anybody's feelings. As if Lucy. . . . but, never mind!

It was Lucy, at any rate, who so unfortunately came into that dreadful talk over the porridge on the morning when the fatal letter came to Euphemia. It arrived just like any other letter. The butler, with his mouth as closely shut as usual, had laid it beside Euphemia's plate. Judging from its large white envelope, nobody could possibly have thought it was as deadly as a poison and sharper than a serpent's tooth. Euphemia opened it, too, just as usual—with her long, lean forefinger, and her eyebrows lifted a little under her grey front of hair. Then she read it—and turned to ice.

It was from her lawyer, or rather from her Four Lawyers, for they all shared the same office, and at the foot of the letter one of them had signed all their four names. It was a pitch-black letter—a thunderbolt. It said at the beginning that the Miss MacKnackeries must expect in future to be a little less well off than they had been in the past, and it said at the end that they were ruined.

You see, Euphemia's grandfather had lent what remained of his £80,000 (after building his great mansion) to the British Government, for the use of the British nation. The British Government of that day put the money into what were called the Consolidated Funds. And to show how much obliged they were to Mr. MacKnackery for the loan of it, they used every year to pay him interest on it—so many shillings for every hundred pounds. Not so much as £4 per annum, as Jean Elspeth had put down in her sum, but as much as they could afford—and that was at least 1,000,000 bawbees. There couldn't have been a safer money-box; nor could Mr. MacKnackery's income have "come in" more regularly if it had come in by clockwork. So far the British Government resembled Stoneyhouse itself.

But the Miss MacKnackeries's father was not only a less imposing man than their grandfather, he had been much less careful of his money. He enjoyed *helping* the nation to use the Funds. He delighted in *buying* things and giving presents, and the more he bought the more he wanted to buy. So he had gradually asked for his money back from the British Government, spending most of it and lending the rest to persons making railways and gasworks in foreign parts, and digging up gold and diamonds, and making scent out of tar, and paint which they said would never wear off or change colour, and everything like that.

These persons paid him for helping them like this a good deal more than the Consolidated Funds could pay him. But then the gasworks are not always so *safe* as the British nation. It is what is called a speculation to lend gentlemen money to help them to dig up diamonds or to make waterworks in Armenia, which means that you cannot be perfectly sure of getting it back again. Often and often, indeed, the Miss MacKnackeries's father had not got *his* money back again.

And now—these long years after his death—the worst had befallen. The four Lawyers had been suddenly compelled to tell the Miss MacKnackeries that nearly every bit left of their grandfather's savings was gone; that their solid gold had vanished like the glinting mists of a June morning. They had for some time been accustomed to growing less and less rich; but that's a very different thing from becoming alarmingly poor. It is the difference between a mouse with a fat nugget of cheese and a mouse with a bread-crumb.

Euphemia, before opening the letter, had put on her pince-nez. As she read, the very life seemed to ebb out of her poor old face, leaving it cold and grey. She finished it to the last word, then with a trembling hand took the glasses off her nose and passed the letter to Tabitha. Tabitha could still read without spectacles. Her light eyes angled rapidly to and fro across the letter, then she, too, put it down, her face not pale, but red and a little swollen. "It is the end, Euphemia," she said.

Jean Elspeth was sitting that morning with her back to the portraits, and at the moment was gently munching a slice of dry toast and Scotch marmalade (made by the Miss MacKnackeries's cook, Mrs. O'Phrump). She had been watching a pied wagtail flitting after flies across the smooth shorn lawn on the white stone terrace. Then her gaze had wandered off to the blue outline of the lovely distant hills, the Grumpy Ones, and her mind had slid into a kind of day-dream.

Into the very middle of this day-dream had broken the sound of Tabitha's words, "It is the end, Euphemia"; and it was as if a trumpet had sounded.

She looked round in dismay, and saw her sisters, Euphemia and Tabitha, sitting there in their chairs at the table, as stiff and cold as statues of stone. Not only this, which was not so very unusual, but they both of them looked extremely unwell. *Then* she noticed the letter. And she knew at once that this must be the serpent that had suddenly bitten her sisters' minds. The blood rushed up into her cheeks, and she said—feeling more intensely sorry for them both than she could possibly express—"Is there anything wrong, Euphemia?"

And Euphemia, in a voice Jean Elspeth would certainly not have recognized if she had heard it from outside the door, replied, "You may well ask it." And then in a rush Jean Elspeth remembered her strange dream of the night before and at once went blundering on: "Well, you know, Euphemia, I had a dream last night, all dark and awful, and, in it, *there* was *Lucy* looking out of a crooked stone window over some water. And she said to me——"

But Tabitha interrupted her: "I think, Elspeth, neither myself nor Euphemia at this moment wish to hear what Lucy, as you call her, said in your dream.

We have received exceedingly bad news this morning, that very closely concerns not only Tabitha and me, but even yourself also. And this is *no* time for frivolity." And it sounded even more tragic in her Scots tongue.

Jean Elspeth had not meant to be frivolous. She had hoped merely, and if but for a moment, to turn her sisters' minds away from this dreadful news that had come with the postman, and to explain what her dream had seemed to promise. But no. It was just her way. Whenever she said anything to anyone—anything that came from the very bottom of her heart, she always made a muddle of it. It sounded as small and meaningless as the echo of a sparrow's cheeping against a bare stone wall. They would look at her out of their green-grey eyes, down their long pale noses, with an expression either grim or superior, or both. Of course, too, at such a moment, any mention of Lucy was a dreadfully silly mistake. Even at the best of times they despised Jean Elspeth for her "childishness". What must they think of her now!

For there never was and there never could be any *real* Lucy. It was only a name. And yet Jean Elspeth still longed to find *some* word of hope or comfort that would bring back a little colour into poor Euphemia's cheeks, and make her look a little less like an image in marble. But no word came. She had even failed to hear what her sisters were saying. At last she could bear herself no longer.

"I am sure, Euphemia, that you would like to talk the letter over with Tabitha in quiet, and that you will tell me if I can be of any help. I think I will go out into the garden."

Euphemia bowed her head. And though, by trying to move with as little noise as possible, Jean Elspeth made her heavy chair give a loud screech on the polished floor, she managed to escape at last.

It was a cold, clear, spring morning, and the trees in the distance were now tipped with their first green buds. The gardeners were already mapping out their rows of plants in the "arbaceous borders", in preparation for the summer. There never was a garden "kept" so well. The angles of the flower-beds on the lawn—diamonds and lozenges, octagons, squares, and oblongs—were as sharp as if they had been cut out of cardboard with a pair of scissors. Not a blade of grass was out of place.

If even one little round pebble pushed up a shoulder in the gravel path, up came a vast cast-iron roller and ground him back into his place. As for a weed, let but one poke its little green bonnet above the black mould, it would soon see what happened.

The wide light from the sky streamed down upon the house, and every single window in the high white wall of it seemed to be scornfully watching Jean Elspeth as she made her way down to a little straight green seat under the terrace. Here, at least, she would be out of their sight.

She sat down, folded her hands in her lap, and looked straight in front of her. She always so sat when she was in trouble. In vain she tried to compose and fix her mind and to *think*. It was impossible. For she had not been there more than a moment or two before her heart knew that Lucy was haunting somewhere close beside her. So close and so much on purpose, it seemed, that it was almost as if she wanted to whisper something in her ear.

Now it has been said that Lucy was only a name. Yet, after all, she was a little more than that. Years and years ago, when Jean Elspeth was only seven, she had "sort of" made Lucy up. It was simply because there was no one else to play with, for Tabitha was five years older, and at least fifty-five times more sensible and intelligent and grown-up. So Jean Elspeth had pretended.

In those days she would sometimes sit on one flower-pot on the long hot or windy terrace, and she would

put another flower-pot for Lucy. And they would talk, or rather she would talk, and Lucy would look. Or sometimes they sat together in a corner of the great bare nursery. And sometimes Jean Elspeth would pretend she was holding Lucy's hand when she fell asleep.

And the really odd thing was that the less in those days she tried to "pretend", the more often Lucy came.

And though Jean Elspeth had never seen her with what is called her naked eye, she must have seen her with some other kind of eye, for she knew that her hair and skin were fairer than the fairest of flax, and that she was dressed in very light and queer-fashioned clothes, though she could not say *how* queer.

Another odd thing was that Lucy always seemed to appear without warning entirely out of nothing, and entirely of herself, when anything mysterious or unexpected or sad or very beautiful happened, and sometimes just before it happened. That had been why she told Euphemia of her dream of the night before. For though everything else in the dream had been dark and dismal, and the water had roared furiously over its rocks, breaking into foam like snow, and Jean Elspeth had been shaken with terror, Lucy herself appearing at the window had been more beautiful than moonlight and as consoling as a star.

It was a pity, of course, that Jean Elspeth had ever even so much as mentioned Lucy at all. But that had been years and years ago, and then she could not really help doing so. For Tabitha had crept up behind her one morning—it was on her eighth birthday—while she herself was sitting in a corner by the large cupboard, with her back to the nursery door, and had overheard her talking to someone.

"Aha! little Miss Toad-in-the-hole! So here you are! And who are *you* talking to?" Tabitha had asked.

Jean Elspeth had turned cold all over. "Nobody," she said.

"Oh, Nobody, is it? Then you just tell me, Madam Skulker, Nobody's name!"

And Jean Elspeth had refused. Unfortunately, she had been wearing that morning a high-waisted frock, with sleeves that came down only to the elbow, and though Tabitha, with nips and pinches of her bare skinny arm, could not make Jean Elspeth cry, she had at least made her tell.

"Oh, so its name's Lucy, is it?" said Tabitha. "You horrid little frump. Then you tell her from me that if *I* catch her anywhere about, I'll scratch her eyes out."

After another pinch or two, and a good "ring-of-the-bells" at Jean Elspeth's plait, Tabitha had gone downstairs to her father.

"Papa," she said, "I am sorry to interrupt you, but I think poor Elspeth must be ill or in a fever. She is 'rambling'. Had we better give her some Gregory's powder, or some castor-oil, do you think?"

Mr. MacKnackery had been worried that morning by a letter about a Gold Mine, something like that which poor Euphemia so many years afterwards was to receive from the Four Lawyers. But when *he* was worried he at once tried to forget his worry. Indeed, even at sight of what looked like an ugly letter, he would begin softly whistling and smiling. So it was almost with a sigh of relief that he pushed the uncomfortable letter into a drawer and climbed the stairs to the nursery.

And when Jean Elspeth, after crying a little as she sat on his knee, had told him about Lucy, he merely smiled out of his dark eyes, and, poking his finger and thumb into a waistcoat pocket, had pulled out, just as if it had been waiting there especially for this occasion, a tiny little gold locket with a picture of a moss-rose inside, which he asked Jean Elspeth to give to Lucy the very next time she came again. "My dear," he had said, "I have my Lucy, too, though I never, never talk about her. I keep her 'for best'."

As for Tabitha, he thanked her most gratefully that morning at luncheon for having been so thoughtful about her sister. "But I fear, my child," he said, "you must be fretting yourself without need. And for fretting there is nothing so good as Gregory's powder. So I have asked Alison to mix a good dose for you at bedtime, and if you are very generous, perhaps Jenny would like to lick the spoon."

The very moment he turned his face away, with as dreadful a grimace as she could manage Tabitha had put out her long pale tongue at Jean Elspeth—which was about as much use as it would have been to put out her tongue for their old doctor, Dr. Menzies—*after* he had gone out of the room.

Even now, years and years after she had become completely grown up, whenever Jean Elspeth thought of those far-away times she always began wool-gathering. And whenever she began wool-gathering Lucy was sure to seem more real to her than at any other time. The gravel path, the green lawn, the distant hills vanished away before her eyes. She was lost as if in a region of light and happiness. There she was happy to be lost. But spattering raindrops on her cheeks soon called her back to herself. A dark cloud had come over the world, and for the first time a foreboding came into her mind of what Euphemia's letter might really mean.

She turned sharply on the little green seat almost as if she had been caught trespassing. And at that instant she could have vowed that she actually saw—this time with her real naked eye—a child standing and looking at her a few paces beyond. It could not have been so, of course; but what most surprised Jean Elspeth was that there should be such a peculiar smile on the child's face—as if she were saying: "Never mind, my dear. Whatever happens, whatever they say, I promise to be with you more than *ever* before. You just see!"

And then, for the very first time in her life, Jean Elspeth felt ashamed of Lucy; and then, still more ashamed of being ashamed. When they were all in such trouble, was it quite fair to Euphemia and Tabitha? She actually went so far as to turn away in the opposite direction, and would have hastened straight back to the house if, at that moment, she had not heard a small, curious fluttering behind her. She glanced swiftly over her shoulder, but it was to find only that a robin had stolen in on her to share her company, and was now eyeing her with his bead-black eye from his perch on the green seat which she had just vacated.

And now, of course, there was no Lucy. Not a trace. She had been "dismissed"—would never come back.

For lunch that day the butler carried in a small soup-tureen of porridge. When he had attended to each of the ladies, and had withdrawn, Euphemia explained to Jean Elspeth precisely what the lawyer's letter meant. It was a long letter, not only about the gentlemen who had failed to find water enough for their waterworks in Armenia, but also about some other gentlemen in Madagascar whose crops of manioc and caoutchouc had been seized with chor-blight. Jean Elspeth did not quite grasp the details; she did not quite understand why the lawyers had ever taken such a fancy to caoutchouc; but she did perfectly understand Euphemia's last sentence: "So you see, Elspeth, we—that is Us—are ruined!"

And would you believe it? Once more Jean Elspeth said the wrong thing. Or rather it was her voice that was wrong. For far away in it was the sound as of a bugle rejoicing at break of day. "And does that mean, Euphemia, that we shall have to *leave* Stoneyhouse?"

"It means," said Tabitha tartly, "that Stoneyhouse may have to leave *us*."

"In either case we are powerless," added Euphemia. And the tone in which Euphemia uttered these words—sitting there straight and erect, with her long white face, in her sleek grey silk morning-gown with its pattern of tiny mauve flowers—brought tears, not to Jean Elspeth's eyes, but to somewhere deep down inside her. It was as if somebody was drawing water out of the very well of her heart.

"It is the *disgrace*," said Tabitha. "To have to turn our backs, to run away. We shall be the talk, the laughing-stock of the county."

"What! Laugh at us because we are ruined!" cried Jean Elspeth.

But this time Tabitha ignored her. "This is the house," she said, "our noble grandfather built for us. And here I will die, unless I am positively driven out of it by these systematic blood-suckers."

"Tabitha!" pleaded Euphemia. "Surely we should not demean ourselves so far as even to call them by their right name."

"Systematic blood-suckers," cried Tabitha fiercely. "I will sell the very rings off my fingers rather than be an exile from the house where I was born. And *he—he* at least shall never witness the ruin into which our father's folly has betrayed us."

She rose from the table, and mounting one of the expensive damask chairs that, unless guests were present, were accustomed to stand in a stately row along the wall, she succeeded, after one or two vain attempts, in turning the immense gilt-framed portrait of her grandfather with its face to the wall.

Then tears really came into Jean Elspeth's eyes. But they were tears of anger rather than of pity. "I think," she said, "that is being dreadfully unkind to Father."

"By this time," said Tabitha sternly, "I should have supposed that you would have given up the notion that you are capable of 'thinking'. What right have you to defend your father, pray, simply because you take after him?"

Jean Elspeth made no answer. Her father at any rate continued to smile at her from *his* nail—though it was not a very good portrait, because the painter had been unable to get the hair and the waistcoat quite right. And if—even at this unhappy moment—Jean Elspeth had had her porridge spoon in her hand, she would certainly have given it a little secret wave in his direction.

But he was not to smile down for very long. The Miss MacKnackeries's grandfather continued to hang with his face to the wall. But the two other portraits, together with the wardrobes, coffers, presses, sideboards, bead-mats, samplers, and even the Indian workboxes, were all taken off in a few weeks, to be sold for what they would fetch. And Euphemia now, instead of five, wore but one ring, and that of turquoises.

In a month all the servants, from the butler to Sally McGullie, and all the gardeners were gone. Mrs. O'Phrump alone remained—first because she was too stout to be likely to be comfortable in any new place, and next, because she wasn't greedy about wages. That was all. Just Mrs. O'Phrump and the gardener's boy, Tom Piper, whose mother lived in the village, and who slept at home. But he was a lazy boy, was Tom Piper, and when he was not fast asleep in the tool-shed, he was loafing in the deserted orchard.

Nevertheless, it was from this moment that Jean Elspeth seemed to have become completely alive.

It was extraordinary to find herself so much herself in so empty a house. The echoes! Why, if you but walked alone along a corridor, you heard your own footsteps pit-a-pattering after you all the way down. If by yourself, in "your ain, ain companie," you but laughed out in a room, it was like being the muffled clapper of a huge hollow bell. All Stoneyhouse seemed endlessly empty now; and perhaps the emptiest place of all was the coach-house.

And then the stables. It was simply astonishing how quickly stray oats, that had fallen by chance into the crannies, sprang up green among the cobble-stones in front of their walls. And if for a little while you actually stood in the stables beside one of the empty mangers, the call of a bird was as shrill as early cock-crow. And you could almost see ghostly horses with their dark eyes looking round at you out of their long narrow heads, as if to say: "So this is what you have done for us!"

Not that Jean Elspeth had very much time to linger over such little experiences. No; and she seemed to have grown even smaller in the empty house. But she was ten times more active. And, though she tried not to be selfish by showing it, she was more than ten times happier. Between Jean Elspeth herself and the eagle-surmounted gateposts, indeed, she now secretly confessed that she had always hated Stoneyhouse. How very odd, then, that the moment it ceased to be a place in which *any* fine personage would be proud to be offered a pillow, she began to be friends with it. She began to pity it.

No doubt Tabitha was right. Their grandfather would assuredly have "turned in his grave," poor creature, at the sound of those enormous vans, those hideous pantechnicons, as their wheels ground down the gravel in the lingering twilight evenings. And yet, after all, that grandfather had been born—a fact that very much shocked Tabitha, whenever her father had smilingly related it—their grandfather had been born in a two-roomed cottage so cramped that, if only you could have got it through the windows, it would have fitted quite comfortably even into the breakfast-room of the great house he had lived to build.

Then there had been not two bawbees in his breeches pocket, and—having been such a good man, as both Euphemia and Tabitha agreed, he did not need a bawbee now. *Would* he then—once the pantechnicons were out of the way—would he, thought Jean Elspeth, have been so very miserable to see all this light and sunshine in the house and to listen to these entrancing echoes.

There were other advantages, too. It was easy to sweep the dining-room now; and much easier to dust it. And one day, more out of kindness than curiosity, after busily whisking over its gilt frame with her feather cornice-broom, Jean Elspeth climbed on to a chair, and, tilting it, looked in at the portrait. A spider had spun its web in one corner, but otherwise (it was almost disappointing) the picture was unchanged. Nor had Mr. MacKnackery yet taken his watch out of his pocket, even though (for his three granddaughters at any rate) the time was now—well, a good way past a-quarter-to-twelve.

Jean Elspeth had had ridiculous thoughts like these as long as she could remember. But now they came swarming into her mind like midsummer bees into a hive. Try as she might, she could not keep them all to herself, and though on this account alone Tabitha seemed to dislike her more than ever, Euphemia seemed sometimes to wish for her company. But then, Euphemia was by no means well. She had begun to stoop a little, and sometimes did not hear what was said to her. To watch her visibly grow older like this gave Jean Elspeth dreadful anxiety. Still, in most things—and she all but said it out loud every morning at her first early look out of her upper window—she was far happier than when Stoneyhouse stood in all its glory. It seemed rather peculiar, but it was true.

Also, there was no time to be anything else; and even if there had been a complete cupboard *full* of neat packages of time *saved*, she would have used them all up in a week. Euphemia, being so poorly, did very little. She helped to make the beds and with the mending. Only the mending, for, fortunately, the making of any new clothes would be unnecessary for years and years to come; they had so many old ones. Tabitha did what she could manage of the lighter work, but although she had a quick tongue, she had slow, clumsy hands. And it is quite certain, though nobody, naturally, would have been so unkind as to say so, that she would never have got even as low wages as Sally McGullie, if she had been in need of a place.

Mrs. O'Phrump did the cooking; but sat on a chair in the kitchen for so many hours together that she became almost like a piece of furniture herself—the heaviest piece in the house. For the cooking of water-porridge and potatoes does not require very much time, and these were now pretty much all that the Miss MacKnackeries had to eat, except for the eggs from Jean Elspeth's three Cochin-Chinas. And Mrs. O'Phrump needed most of these, as there was so much of her to sustain. As for the apples and pears in the orchard, since Mrs. O'Phrump was too stout to stoop to make dumplings, Jean Elspeth, having two wonderful rows of small sharp teeth, shared these raw with Tom Piper —though *he* had all the stomachaches.

All the rest of the work fell to Jean Elspeth. She slaved from morning till night. And to slave the more merrily, she had taught herself to whistle. She never asked herself why she was so happy. And no doubt it was chiefly by contrast with having been so cramped in, and kept under, and passed over in days gone by.

Still, certain things did now happen in Stoneyhouse that had not happened before, and some of these may have helped. For one thing, Jean Elspeth had always dreaded "company". Dressing-up made her feel awkward. The simplest stranger made her shy. She would have much preferred to say Boh to a goose. None came now, except Dr. Menzies, who of his kindness sometimes called to feel Euphemia's pulse and mutter, "H'm h'm"—though he did not charge for it.

Jean Elspeth, too, had never liked servants, not because they were servants, but because Euphemia and Tabitha seemed to think they oughtn't to be talked to much. Just given their orders. Now Jean Elspeth could easily have given everything else in the world: but not orders. And if there ever *had* been an interesting creature in Stoneyhouse, even though she was so stupid in some things, it was Sally McGullie.

Then, again, Jean Elspeth, being by nature desperately untidy, never showed it now. For it's all but impossible to be untidy in a room that contains only a table and three chairs!

Then, yet again, Jean Elspeth, before the gentlemen in Armenia and Madagascar had been disappointed in their waterworks and caoutchouc, had had very little to do. She was scarcely even allowed to read. For Tabitha was convinced that most reading was a waste of time, and trash at that; while improving books had never the least bit improved Jean Elspeth. But now she had so many things to do that it was a perfect joy to fit them all in (like the pieces of a puzzle). And the perfectest joy of all was to scramble into her truckle bed, which had formerly been Sally McGullie's bed, and, with a tallow candle stuck by its own grease to the left-hand knob, to read and read and read.

The hours she spent like this, with no living company but roving mice and flitting moths and, in autumn, perhaps a queen wasp. When her upper parts grew cold in winter weather, she spread her skirt over the quilt. One thin blanket, indeed, is not much comfort on cold nights when one is lying up North there, almost in positive view of the Grumpy Ones. As for her feet, she used to boil some water in the great solitary kitchen in a kettle and fill a wine-bottle.

This, of course, broke a good many bottles; and it was an odd thing that until there was only one left, Tabitha (whose feet were like slabs of ice) refused to hear of anything so vulgar. And *then* she changed her mind. And medicine-bottles are too small.

Apart from all this, queer things now happened in Stoneyhouse. Little things, but entrancing. The pantechnicon men, for example, had broken a window on a lower staircase as they were heaving down old Mr. MacKnackery's best wardrobe. A sweetheart pair of robins in the springtime noticed this hole, and decided to build their nest in a nook of the cornice. Jean Elspeth (with her tiny whistling) was accepted as the bosom friend of the whole family.

There was, too, a boot cupboard, one too far from the kitchen for Mrs. O'Phrump to range. Its window had been left open. And when, by chance, Jean Elspeth looked in one sunny afternoon, there hung within it a marvellous bush of Traveller's Joy, rather pale in leaf, but actually flowering there; and even a butterfly sipping of its nectar. After that, not a day passed now but she would peep in at this delicate green visitor, and kiss her hand. It was, too, an immense relief to Jean Elspeth to have said good-bye for ever to lots of things in the house that seemed to her to have been her enemies ever since she was five years old.

She wandered up into rooms she had never seen before, and looked out of windows whose views had never before lain under her eyes. Nor did she cease to day-dream, but indulged in only tiny ones that may come and go, like swifts, between two ticks of a clock. And although, of course, Tabitha strongly disapproved of much that delighted Jean Elspeth now, there was not nearly so much time in which to tell her so.

Besides, Jean Elspeth was more useful in that great barracks of a place than ten superior parlour-maids would have been. She was much more like a steam-engine than a maiden lady. And, like a steam-engine, she refused to be angry; she refused to sulk; and she usually refused to answer back. When nowadays, however, she *did* answer back, her tongue had a sting to it at least as sharp (though never so venomous) as that of the busy bee.

And last, but no less, there was the *outside* of the house. As soon as ever Mr. McPhizz and his under-gardeners had departed with their shears and knives and edging-irons and mowing machines, wildness had begun to creep into the garden. Wind and bird carried in seeds from the wilderness, and after but two summers, the trim barbered lawns sprang up into a marvellous meadow of daisies and buttercups, dandelions, meadowsweet and fools' parsley, and then dock, thistle, groundsel and feathery grasses. Ivy, hop, briony, convolvulus crept across the terrace; Hosts of the Tiny blossomed between the stones. Moss, too, in mats and cushions of a green livelier than the emerald, or even than a one-night-old beech-leaf. Rain stains now softly coloured the white walls, as if a stranger had come in the night and begun to paint pictures there. And the roses, in their now hidden beds, rushed back as fast as ever they could to bloom like their wild-briar sisters again.

And not only green things growing. Jean Elspeth would tiptoe out to see complete little immense families of rabbits nibbling their breakfast or supper of dandelion leaves on the very flagstones under the windows. Squirrels nutted; moles burrowed; hedgehogs came beetle-hunting; mice of every tiny size scampered and twinkled and danced and made merry.

As for the birds—birds numberless! And of so many kinds and colours and notes that she had to sit up half the night looking out their names in the huge bird-book her father had given her on her eleventh Christmas. This was the one treasure she had saved from the pantechnicon men. She had wrapped it up in two copies of the *Scotsman*, and hidden it in the chimney. She felt a little guilty over it at times, but none the less determined that the Four Lawyers should never hear of *that*.

It was strange, exceedingly strange, to be so happy; and Jean Elspeth sometimes could hardly contain herself, she was so much ashamed of it in the presence of her sisters. Still, she drew the line, as they say, at Lucy.

And that was the strangest and oddest thing of all. After the dreadful shock of the Four Lawyers' letter, after the torment and anxiety and horror, the pantechnicons and the tradespeople, poor Tabitha and

Euphemia—however brave their faces and stiff their backs—had drooped within like flowers in autumn nipped by frost. In their pride, too, they had renounced even the friends who would have been faithful to them in their trouble.

They shut themselves up in themselves more than ever, like birds in cages. They scarcely ever even looked from the windows. It was only on Sundays they went out of doors. Euphemia, too, had sometimes to keep her bed. And Jean Elspeth would cry to herself, "Oh, my dear! oh, my dear!" at the sight of Tabitha trailing about the house with a large duster and so little to dust. To see her sipping at her water-porridge as if she were not in the least hungry, as if it was the daintiest dish in Christendom, was like having a knife stuck in one's very breast.

Yet, such was Tabitha's "strength of mind" and hardihood, Jean Elspeth never dared to comfort her, to cheer her up, to wave her spoon by so much as a quarter of an inch in *her* direction.

In these circumstances it had seemed to Jean Elspeth it would be utterly unfair to share Lucy's company, even in her hidden mind. It would be like stealing a march, as they say. It would be cheating. At any rate, it might hurt their feelings. They would see, more stark than ever before, how desolate they were. They would look up and realize by the very light in her eyes that her old playmate had not deserted her. No. She would wait. There was plenty of time. She would keep her wishes down. And the little secret door of her mind should be left, not, as it once was, wide open, but just ajar.

How, she could not exactly say. And yet, in spite of all this, Lucy herself, just as if she were a real live ghost, seemed to be everywhere. If in her scrubbing Jean Elspeth happened to glance up out of the window, as like as not that fair gentle face would be stealthily smiling in. If some moonlight night she leaned for a few precious sweet cold moments over her bedroom sill, as like as not that pale phantom would be seen wandering, shadowless, amid the tall whispering weeds and grasses of the lawn.

Spectres and ghosts, of course, may be the most forbidding company. But Lucy was nothing but gaiety and grace. The least little glimpse of her was like hearing a wild bird singing—even the Southern nightingale, though without those long, bubbling, grievous notes that seem to darken the darkness. Having this ghost, then, for company, however much she tried not to heed it, all that Jean Elspeth *had* to do in order just to play fair—and she did it with all her might—was not to *look* for Lucy, and not to *show* that she saw her, when there she was, plain to be seen, before her very eyes. And when at last she realized her plot was succeeding, that Lucy was gone from her, her very heart seemed to come into her mouth.

And so the years went by. And the sisters became older and older, and Stoneyhouse older and older too. Walls, fences, stables, coach-house, hen-house, and the square lodge crept on steadily to rack and ruin. Tabitha kept more and more to herself, and the sisters scarcely spoke at meal-times.

Then at last Euphemia fell really ill; and everything else for a while went completely out of Jean Elspeth's life and remembrance. She hadn't a moment even to lean from her window or to read in her bed. It was unfortunate, of course, that Euphemia's bedroom was three stair-flights up. Jean Elspeth's legs grew very tired of climbing those long ladders, and Tabitha could do little else but sit at the window and knit—knit the wool of worn-out shawls and stockings into new ones. So she would stay for hours together, never raising her eyes to glance over the pair of horn-rimmed spectacles that had belonged to her grandfather, and now straddled her own lean nose. Dr. Menzies, too, was an old man now, and could visit them very seldom.

Jean Elspeth herself seldom even went to bed. She sat on a chair in Euphemia's room and snatched morsels of sleep, as a hungry dog snatches at bits of meat on a butcher's tray. It was on such a night as this, nodding there in her chair, that, after having seemed to fall into a long narrow nightmare hole of utter cold and darkness, and to have stayed there for centuries without light or sound, she was suddenly roused by Euphemia's voice.

It was not Euphemia's usual voice, and the words were following one another much more rapidly than usual, like sheep and lambs running through a gate. Daybreak was at the window. And in this first chill eastern light Euphemia was sitting up in bed—a thing she had been unable to do for weeks. And she was asking Jean Elspeth to tell her who the child was that was now standing at the end of her bed.

Euphemia described her, too—"A fair child with straight hair. And she is carrying a bundle of gorse, with its prickles and flowers wide open. I can mell the almond smell. And she keeps on looking and smiling first at me, and then at you. Don't you *see*, Elspeth? Tell her, please, to go away. Tell her I don't want to be happy like that. She is making me afraid. Tell her to go away at once, please."

Jean Elspeth sat shivering, colder than a snail in its winter shell. The awful thing was to know that this visitor must be Lucy, and yet not to be able to see her—not a vestige, nothing but the iron bed and the bed-post, and Euphemia sitting there, just gazing. How, then, could she tell Lucy to go away?

She scurried across the room, and took Euphemia's cold hands in hers. "You are dreaming, Euphemia. *I* see nothing. And if it is a pleasant dream, why drive it away?"

"No," said Euphemia, in the same strange, low, clear voice. "It is not a dream. You are deceiving me, Elspeth. She has come only to mock at me. Send her away!"

And Jean Elspeth, gazing into her sister's wide light eyes, that now seemed deeper than the deepest well that ever was on earth, was compelled to answer her.

"Please, please, Euphemia, do not think of it any more. There is nothing to fear—nothing at all. Why, it sounds like Lucy—that old silly story; do you remember? But I have not seen her myself for ever so long. I *couldn't* while you are ill."

The lids closed gently down over the wide eyes, but Euphemia still held tight to Jean Elspeth's work-roughened hand. "Never mind, then," she whispered, "if that is all. I had no wish to take her away from you, Elspeth. Keep close to me. One thing, we are happier now, you and I."

"Oh, Euphemia, do you mean that?" said Jean Elspeth, peering closer.

"Well," Euphemia replied; and it was as if there were now two voices speaking: the old Euphemia's and this low, even, dreamlike voice. "I mean it. There is plenty of air now—a different place. And I hope your friend will come as often as she pleases. There's room for us all."

And with that word "room", and the grim smile that accompanied it, all the old Euphemia seemed to have come back again, though a moment after she dropped back upon her pillow and appeared to be asleep.

Seeing her thus quiet once more, Jean Elspeth very, very cautiously turned her head. The first rays of the sun were on the window. Not the faintest scent of almond was borne to her nostrils on the air. There was no sign at all of any company. A crooked frown had settled on her forehead. She was cold through and through, and her body ached; but she tried to smile, and almost imperceptibly lifted a finger just as if it held a teaspoon and she was waving it in her own old secret childish way to her father's portrait on the wall.

Now and again after that Jean Elspeth watched the same absent far-away look steal over Euphemia's face, and the same fixed smile, dour and grim, and yet happy—like still deep water under waves. It was almost as if Euphemia were amused at having stolen Lucy away.

"You see, my dear," she said suddenly one morning, as if after a long talk, "it only proves that we all go the same way home."

"Euphemia, please don't say that," whispered Jean Elspeth.

"But why not?" said Euphemia. "So it is. And *she* almost laughing out loud at me. The hussy!" . . .

None of their old friends knew when Euphemia died, so it was only Dr. Menzies and his sister who came to Stoneyhouse for the funeral. And though Jean Elspeth would now have been contented to do *all* the work in the house and to take care of Tabitha and her knitting into the bargain, they persuaded her at last that this would be impossible. And so, one blazing hot morning, having given a little parting gift to Tom

Piper and wept a moment or two on Mrs. O'Phrump's ample shoulder, Jean Elspeth climbed with Tabitha into a cab, and that evening found herself hundreds of miles away from Stoneyhouse, in the two upper rooms set apar for the two ladies by Sally McGullie, who had married a fisherman and was now Mrs. John Jones.

Jean Elspeth could not have imagined a life so different. It was as if she had simply been pulled up by the roots. Whenever Tabitha could spare her—and that was seldom now—she would sit at her window looking on the square stone harbour and the sea, or in a glass shelter on its narrow front. But now that time stretched vacantly before her, and she was at liberty if she pleased to "pretend" whenever she wished, and to fall into day-dreams one after another just as they might happen to come, it was life's queer way that she could scarcely picture Lucy now, even with her inward eye, and never with her naked one.

It was, too, just the way of this odd world that she should pine and long for Stoneyhouse beyond words to tell. She felt sometimes she must die—suffocate—of homesickness, and would frown at the grey moving sea, as if that alone were the enemy who was keeping her away from it. Not only this, but she saved up in a tin money-box every bawbee which she could spare of the little money the Four Lawyers had managed to save from the caoutchouc. And all for one distant purpose.

And at length, years and years afterwards, she told Mrs. Jones that she could bear herself no longer, that —like the cat in the fairy-tale—she must pay a visit, and must go alone. . . .

It was on an autumn afternoon, about five o'clock, and long shadows were creeping across the grasses of the forsaken garden when Jean Elspeth came into sight again of Stoneyhouse, and found herself standing some little distance from the gaunt familiar walls by a dank pond that had formed itself in a hollow of the garden. Her father had delighted in water, and, putting to use a tiny stream that coursed near by had made a jetting

fountain and a fishpond. The fountain having long ceased to flow and the pond having become choked with water-weeds, the stream had pushed its way out across the hollows, and had made itself this last dark resting-place. You might almost have thought it was trying to copy Jean Elspeth's life in Sallie Jones's sea-side cottage. On the other hand, the windows of the great house did not stare so fiercely now; they were blurred and empty, like the eyes of a man walking in his sleep. One of the chimney-stacks had toppled down, and creepers had rambled all over the wide expanse of the walls.

Jean Elspeth, little old woman that she now was, in her dingy black bonnet and a beaded mantle that had belonged to Euphemia, stood there drinking the great still scene in, as a dry sponge drinks in salt water.

And after hesitating for some little time, she decided to venture nearer. She pushed her way through the matted wilderness of the garden, crossed the terrace, and presently peered in through one of the dingy dining-room windows. Half a shutter had by chance been left unhasped. When her eyes were grown accustomed to the gloom within, she discovered that the opposite wall was now quite empty. The portrait of her grandfather must have slowly ravelled through its cord. It had fallen face upwards on to the boards beneath.

It saddened her to see this. She had left the picture hanging there simply because she felt sure that Euphemia would so have wished it to hang. But though she wearied herself out seeking to find entry into the house, in order, at least, to lean her grandfather up again against the wall, it was in vain. The doors were rustily bolted; the lower windows tight—shut. And it was beginning to be twilight when she found herself once more beside the cold stagnant pool.

All this while she had been utterly alone. It had been a dreadful and sorrowful sight to see the great house thus decaying, and all this neglect. Yet she was not unhappy, for it seemed with its trees and greenery in this solitude to be uncomplaining and at peace. And so, too, was she. It was as if her whole life had just vanished and flitted away like a dream, leaving merely her body standing there in the evening light under the boughs of the great green chestnut-tree overhead.

And then by chance, in that deep hush, her eyes wandered to the surface of the water at her feet, and there fixed themselves, her whole mind in a sudden confusion. For by some curious freak of the cheating dusk, she saw gazing back at her from under a squat old crape bonnet, with Euphemia's cast-off beaded mantle on the shoulders beneath it, a face not in the least like that of the little old woman inside them, but a face, fair and smiling, as of one eternally young and happy and blessed—Lucy's. She gazed and gazed, in the darkening evening. A peace beyond understanding comforted her spirit. It was by far the oddest thing that had ever happened to Jean Elspeth in all the eighty years of her odd long life on earth.

Alice's Godmother

Though Alice sat steadily looking out of the small square pane of glass in the railway carriage, she was not really seeing the green and hilly country through which the train now clattered on its way. While everything near—quickening hedges, grazing cattle, galloping calves, wood, farm and stony foaming brook—swept past far too swiftly for more than a darting glance; everything in the distance—hill, tree and spire—seemed to be stealthily wheeling forward, as if to waylay the puffing engine and prevent it from reaching her journey's end.

"If only it would!" sighed Alice to herself. "How much—much happier I should be!" Her blue eyes widened at the fancy. Then once more a frown of anxiety drew her eyebrows together; but she said nothing aloud. She sat on in her corner gently clasping her mother's hand and pondering in dismay on what might happen to her in the next few hours.

Alice and her mother a little prided themselves on being just "two quiet ordinary people", happy in each other's company, and very seldom going out or paying calls and visits. And the particular visit that Alice was about to make when they reached the little country station of Freshing, she was to make alone. It was this that alarmed her. The invitation in that queer scrabbling handwriting had been to herself only. So though her mother was with her now, soon they would be parting.

And every now and again Alice would give the hand she held in hers a gentle squeeze of self-reassurance. It was the Good-bye—though it would be only for a few hours—that she dreaded.

And yet their plans had all been talked over and settled again and again. Alice must, of course, take a fly from the station—whatever the expense. After telling the cabman when she would need him again, she

would get into it and her mother would wait for her in a room at the village Inn until she herself returned in the early evening from her visit. Then everything would be safely over. And to imagine the joy of seeing all these fields and woods come racing back the other way round almost made Alice ill.

It was absurd to be so nervous. Alice had told herself that a hundred times. But it was no use. The very thought of her great-great-great-great-great-great-

great-great-grandmother filled her heart with a continuous foreboding. If only she were a little stronger-minded; if only this old old lady, who was also her god-mother, had asked her mother to come with her; if only her heart would stop beating so fast; if only a wheel would come off the engine!

But then, after all, Alice had never before so much as seen her godmother. Even now she could not be quite certain that she had the number of "greats" to the "grandmama" quite right. Not even strong-minded people, she supposed, are often suddenly invited to tea with relatives aged three-hundred-and-forty-nine. And not only that either; for this day—this very Saturday—was her godmother's birthday: her three-hundred-and-fiftieth!

Whenever Alice remembered this, a faint smile stole into her face. At seventeen a birthday is a real "event". Life is galloping on. You are sprouting up like a beanstalk. Your hair is "put up" (or at least it was when Alice was a girl), your skirts "come down", and you're soon to "come out". In other words you are beginning to be really and truly grown-up. But three-hundred-and-fifty! Surely by that time. . . . It must be difficult even to be certain you have the total right. Surely there can't be *any* kind of a change by then. Surely not!

Still, Alice thought, it is perhaps the *name* of the number that chiefly counts. She herself had known what an odd shock it had been to slip into her teens, and could guess what the shivers would be like of the plunge into her twenties. Yet even if it were only the name of the number—why, at the end of three centuries you must be beginning to be getting accustomed to birthdays.

It was a little odd that her godmother had never asked to see her before. Years ago she had sent her a squat parcel-gilt mug—a mug that her godmother herself used to drink her beer out of when she was a child of ten in Queen Elizabeth's reign. A little sheepskin, illuminated Prayer Book, too, that had once been given to her godmother by Charles the First, and a few exquisite little old gold trinkets had come too. But receiving presents is not the same thing as actually meeting and talking with the mysterious giver of them. It is one thing to imagine the unknown; another thing altogether to meet it face to face. What would her godmother look like? What *could* she look like? Alice hadn't the faintest notion. Old ladies of eighty and upwards are not unusual; but you can't just multiply eighty by four as if growing older were merely a sum in arithmetic.

Perhaps when you are very old indeed, Alice suspected, you have no wish left to sit for a portrait or to be photographed. It is a petrifying experience even when you are young. When you are—well, very old indeed, you may prefer to—well, to keep yourself *to* yourself. *She* would.

"Mamma dear," she suddenly twisted round on her hard seat, her straight ribboned straw-coloured hair slipping over in one smooth ripple on her shoulder as she did so; "Mamma dear, I can't think even now what I ought to do when I go into the room. Will there be anybody there, do you think? Do I shake hands? I suppose she won't kiss me? I simply can't think what I ought to do. I shall just hate leaving you—being left, I mean."

She stroked hard with her fingers the hand that was in her own, and as she gazed at her mother's face in this increasing anxiety, she knew that the smile on it was just like a pretty blind over a window, and that her mother's self within was almost as much perturbed over this visit as she was herself.

"It's getting nearer, darling, at any rate, isn't it?" her mother whispered. "So it will sooner be over." Whereupon the fat old farmer in the further corner of the carriage emitted yet another grunt. He was fast asleep. "I *think*," her mother continued softly, "I should first enquire of the maid if she is quite well—your godmother, I mean, my dear. Say, 'Do you think Miss Cheyney is well enough to see me?' She will know what you ought to do. I am not even certain whether the poor old lady can speak; though her handwriting is simply marvellous."

"But Mummie darling, how are we to know that there *will* be a maid? Didn't they, in godmother's time, always have 'retainers'? Supposing there are rows of them in the hall! And when ought I to get up to say Good-bye? If she is deaf and blind *and* dumb I really don't know what I *shall* do!"

A dozen questions at least like this had been asked but not answered during the last few days, and although Alice's cheek, with that light hair, was naturally pale, her mother watched it grow paler yet as the uncomfortable old-fashioned railway-carriage they sat in jogged steadily on its way.

"Whenever I am in any difficulty, sweetheart," she whispered close up to her daughter's ear, "I always say a little prayer."

"Yes, yes, dear dearest," said Alice, gazing at the fat old farmer, fast asleep. "But if only I weren't going quite alone! I don't think, you know, she can be a very good godmother: she never said a word in her letter about my Confirmation. She's at least old enough to know better." Once more the ghost of a smile stole softly over her face. But she clasped her mother's fingers even a little tighter, and the hedges and meadows continued to sidle by.

They said Good-bye to one another actually inside the cab, so as to be out of sight of the Inn and the cabman.

"I expect, my sweet," breathed Alice's mother, in the midst of this long embrace, "we shall both soon be smiling away like two turtledoves at the thought of all our worry. We can't tell what kind things she may not be thinking of, can we? And don't forget, I shall be waiting for you in the 'Red Lion'—there's the sign, my dear, as you see. And if there is time, perhaps we will have a little supper there all to ourselves—a little soup, if they have it; or at any rate, an egg. I don't suppose you will have a very *substantial* tea. Not in the circumstances. But still, your godmother wouldn't have asked you to visit her if she had not really wanted to see you. We mustn't forget that, darling."

Alice craned her head out of the window till her mother was out of sight behind the hedge. And the fly rolled gently on and on and on along the dusty lanes in the direction of the Grange. On and on and on. Surely, thought Alice at last, we must have gone miles and miles. At this she sprang up and thrust her head out of the window, and called up to the cabman, "The Grange, you know, please."

"That's it, Miss, the Grange," he shouted back, with a flourish of his whip. "Not as how I can take you into the Park, Miss. It ain't allowed."

"Mercy me," sighed Alice as she sank back on the fusty blue cushions. "Supposing there are miles of avenue, and the front door's at the back!"

It was a pleasant sunny afternoon. The trim hedgerows were all in their earliest green; and the flowers of spring—primroses, violets, jack-in-the-hedge, stitchwort—in palest blossom starred the banks. It was only half-past three by Alice's little silver watch. She would be in good time, then. In a few minutes, indeed, the fly drew up beside immense rusty wrought-iron gates on the four posts of which stood heavy birds in stone, with lowered heads, brooding with outstretched wings.

"And you will be sure to come back for me at six?" Alice implored the cabman, though she tried to keep her voice natural and formal. "Not a minute later than six, please. And then wait here until I come."

The cabman ducked his head and touched his hat; drew his old horse round in the shafts, and off he went. Alice was alone.

With one last longing look at the strange though friendly country lane—and there was not a house in sight—Alice pushed open the little gate at the side of the two large ones. It emitted a faint, mocking squeal as it turned slowly upon its hinges. Beyond it rose a hedge of yew at least twenty feet high, and in a nook there stood a small square lodge, its windows shuttered, a scurry of dead leaves in its ancient porch. Alice came to a standstill. This was a difficulty neither she nor her mother had foreseen. Ought she to knock or to go straight on? The house looked as blind as a bat. She stepped back, and glanced up at the chimneys. Not the faintest plume of smoke was visible against the dark foliage of the ilex behind the house. Some unseen bird flew into the shadows with a cry of alarm.

Surely the lodge was empty. None the less it might be good manners to make sure, so she stepped into the porch and knocked—but knocked in vain. After pausing a minute or two, and scanning once more the lifeless windows, in a silence broken only by the distant laughing of a woodpecker, Alice determined to go on.

So thick and close were the tufted mosses in the gravel of the narrow avenue that her footsteps made no sound. So deep was the shade cast by the immense trees that grew on either side she could have fancied evening was already come, though it was yet early afternoon. Mammoth beeches lifted their vast boughs into the air; the dark hollows in their ancient boles capacious enough for the dwelling-house of a complete family of humans. In the distance Alice could see between their branches gigantic cedars, and others still further, beneath which grazed what she supposed was a herd of deer, though it was impossible to be quite certain from so far.

The few wild creatures which had long ago detected her in these haunts were strangely tame. They did not trouble to run away; but turned aside and watched her as she passed, the birds hopping a little further out of her reach while yet continuing on their errands. In sheer curiosity indeed Alice made an attempt to get as near as she possibly could to a large buck rabbit that sat nibbling under the broken rail of the fence. With such success that he actually allowed her to scratch his furry head and stroke his long lopping ears.

"Well," thought she with a sigh as she straightened herself, "there can't be very much to be afraid of in great-great-great-great-great-great-great-great-grand-mother's house if the rabbits are as tame as all that. *Au revoir*," she whispered to the creature; "I hope to see you again very very soon." And on she went.

Now and then a hunchbacked thorn-tree came into view, and now and then a holly. Alice had heard long ago that hollies are wise enough not to grow prickles where no animal can damage their leaves by browsing on them. These hollies seemed to have no prickles at all, and the hawthorns, in spite of their bright green coats, speckled with tight buds, were almost as twisted out of shape as if mischievous little boys had tied knots in them when they were saplings. But how sweet was the tranquil air. So sweet indeed that this quiet avenue with its towering branches and the child-like blue of the skies overhead pacified her mind, and she had almost forgotten her godmother when, suddenly, at a break between the trees there came into view a coach.

Not exactly a coach, perhaps, but a large painted carriage of a faded vermilion and yellow, drawn by two cream-coloured horses—a coachman on the box in a mulberry livery, and a footman beside him. What was really strange, this conveyance was being noiselessly driven round a circular track so overgrown with moss and weeds that it was hardly discernible against the green of the grass. Alice could not but watch it come nearer and nearer—as she stood drawn up close to the furrowed bark of an oak that branched overhead. This must be her godmother's carriage. She must be taking her daily drive in concealment from the wide wide world. But no: it had drawn near; and now, with a glimpse of the faded red morocco within, it had passed; it was empty. Only the backs of coachman and footman now showed above its sun-bleached panels—their powdered hair, their cockaded hats.

All Alice's misgivings winged back into her mind at sight of this unusual spectacle. She tiptoed out of her hiding-place, and hastened on. Her one wish now was to reach her journey's end. Presently after, indeed, the House itself appeared in sight. The shorn flowerless sward gently sloped towards its dark low walls and grey chimneys. To the right of it lay a pool as flat as a huge looking-glass in the frame of its trees. Behind it rose a smooth green hill.

Alice paused again behind yet another of the huge grey boles to scan it more closely before she herself could be spied out from any of its many windows. It looked as if it had stood there for ever. It looked as if its massive stones had of their own weight been sinking imperceptibly, century after century, into the ground. Not a blossoming shrub, not a flower nearby—except only a powder of daisies and a few yellow dandelions.

Only green turf and trees, and the ancient avenue on which she stood, sweeping gently towards its low-porched entrance. "Well," she sighed to herself, "I'm thankful I don't live *there*, that's all—not even if I were a thousand-and-one!" She drew herself up, glanced at her shoes, gave a little push to her ribboned straw hat, and, with as much dignity as she could manage, proceeded straight onwards.

A hoarse bell responded, after a whole second's pause, to the gentle tug she had given the iron pull that hung in the porch. It cried "Ay, ay!" and fell silent. And Alice continued to look at the immense iron knocker which she hadn't the courage to use.

Without a sound the door opened at last, and there, as she had feared, stood, not a friendly parlour-maid with a neat laundered cap, but an old man in a black tail-coat who looked at her out of his pale grey eyes as if she were a stuffed bird in a glass case. Either he had been shrinking for some little time, or he must surely have put on somebody else's clothes, they hung so loosely on his shoulders.

"I am Miss Alice Cheyney—Miss Alice Cheyney," she said. "I think my great-great . . . Miss Cheyney is expecting me—that is, of course, if she is quite well." These few words had used up the whole of one breath, and her godmother's old butler continued to gaze at her, while they sank into his mind.

"Will you please to walk in," he said at last. "Miss Cheyney bade me express the wish that you will make yourself at home. She hopes to be with you immediately." Whereupon he led the way, and Alice followed him—across a wide hall, lit with low, greenish, stone-mullioned windows. On either side stood suits of burnished armour, with lifted visors. But where the glittering eyes of their long-gone owners once had gleamed, nothing now showed but a little narrow darkness. After a hasty glance or two to either side, Alice kept her eyes fixed on the humped back of the little old butler. Up three polished stairs, under a hanging tapestry, he led her on, and at length, at the end of a long gallery, ushered her into what she supposed was her godmother's sitting-room. There, with a bow, he left her. Alice breathed one long deep sigh, and then, having unbuttoned and buttoned up again one of her grey silk gloves, she sat down on the edge of a chair near the door.

It was a long, low-pitched, but not very wide room, with a moulded ceiling and panelled walls, and never before had Alice seen such furniture. In spite of the dreadful shyness that seemed to fill her to the very brim, at thought of her mother's little pink-and-muslin drawing-room compared with this, she almost burst out laughing.

Make herself at home! Why, any one of those coffers would hide her away for ever, like the hapless young bride in "The Mistletoe Bough". As for the hanging portraits in their great faded frames, though she guessed at once they must be by "old masters", and therefore eyed them as solemnly as she could, she had never supposed human beings could look so odd and so unfriendly. It was not so much their clothes: their stomachers, their slashed doublets and wide velvet caps, but their faces. Ladies with high bald foreheads and tapering fingers and thumb-rings, and men sour and dour and glowering.

"Oho! Miss Nobody!" they seemed to be saying, "And pray what are *you* doing here?"

The one single exception was the drawing of a girl of about her own age. A dainty cap with flaps all but concealed her yellow hair; a necklet dangled at her breast; the primrose-coloured bodice sloped sharply to the waist. So delicate were the lines of this drawing and so faint the tinted chalk, they hardly stained the paper. Yet the eyes that gazed out across the low room at Alice seemed to be alight with life. A smile half-mocking, half-serious, lingered in their depths. See, I am lovely, it seemed to be hinting, and yet how soon to be gone! And even though Alice had never before seen a face so enchanting, she could not but confess it bore a remote resemblance to herself. Why this should have a little restored her confidence she could not tell. None the less, she deliberately smiled back at the drawing as if to say, "Well, my dear, I shall have *you* on my side, whatever happens."

The lagging minutes ticked solemnly by. Not a sound to be heard in the great house; not a footfall. But at last a door at the further end of the room softly opened, and in the greenish light of the deep mullioned window appeared what Alice knew was She.

She was leaning smally on the arm of the butler who had admitted Alice to the house. Quiet as shadows they entered the room; then paused for a moment, while yet another man-servant arranged a chair for his mistress. Meanwhile the old lady was peering steadily in search of her visitor. She must once have been as tall as Alice herself, but now time had shrunken her up into the stature of a child, and though her small head was set firmly on the narrow shoulders, these stooped like the wings of the morose stone birds upon her gates.

"Ah, is that you, my dear?" cried a voice; but so minute was the sound of these words that Alice went suddenly hot all over lest she had merely imagined them.

"I say, is that you, my dear?" repeated the voice. There was no mistaking now. Alice ventured a pace forward into the light, her knees trembling beneath her, and the old lady groped out a hand—its shrunken fingers closed one upon another like the cold claws of a bird.

For an instant Alice hesitated. The dreadful moment was come. Then she advanced, made the old lady a curtsy, and lifted the icy fingers to her lips.

"All I can say *is*," she confided to her mother when they met again, "all I can say *is*, Mamma, if it had been the Pope, I suppose I should have kissed his toe. And really, I would have very much rather."

None the less, Alice's godmother had evidently taken no offence at this gesture. Indeed what Alice thought might be a smile crinkled, as it were, across the exquisite web of wrinkles on her face. On her acorn-shaped head rose a high lace and silver cap resembling the gown she wore; and silk mittens concealed her wrists. She was so small that Alice had to bend almost double over her fingers. And when she was seated in her chair it was as if a large doll sat there—but a marvellous doll that had voice, thought, senses and motion beyond any human artificer's wildest fancy. The eyes in this dry wizened-up countenance—of a much fainter blue than the palest forget-me-not—steadily continued to look at Alice, the while the butler and footman with head inclined stood surveying their mistress. Then, as if at a secret signal, they both bowed and retired.

"Be seated, my dear," the tinkling voice began when they had withdrawn. And there fell a horrifying pause. Alice gazed at the old lady, and like half-transparent glass the aged eyes continued to survey herself, the bird-like hands crossed daintily over the square lace handkerchief held in the narrow lap. Alice grew hotter and hotter. "What a very beautiful old house this is, great-grandmamma," she suddenly blurted out. "And those wonderful trees!"

No flicker of expression showed that Miss Cheyney had heard what she had said. And yet Alice could not help thinking that she *had* heard, and that for some reason she had disapproved of her remark.

"Now come," piped the tiny voice, "now come; tell me what you have been doing this long time. And how is your mother? I think I faintly remember seeing her, my dear, soon after she married your father, Mr. James Beaton."

"Mr. Beaton, I *think*, was my great-grandfather, great-grandmamma," Alice breathed softly. "My father's name, you know, was John—John Cheyney."

"Ah well, your great-*grand*father, to be sure," said the old lady. "I never pay much attention to dates. And has anything been happening lately?"

"Happening, great-grandmamma?" echoed Alice.

"Beyond?" said the old lady. "In the world?"

Poor Alice; she knew well the experience of nibbling a pen over impossible questions in history examinations, but this was far worse than any she had ever encountered.

"There, you see!" continued her godmother, "I hear of the wonderful things they are doing, and yet when I ask a simple question like that no one has anything to say. Have you travelled on one of these steam railway trains yet? Locomotives?"

"I came that way this afternoon, great-grandmamma."

"Ah, I thought you looked a little flushed. The smoke must be most disagreeable."

Alice smiled. "No, thank you," she said kindly.

"And how is Queen Victoria?" said the old lady. "She is still alive?"

"Oh yes, great-grandmamma. And that is just, of course, what *has* been happening. It's her Diamond Jubilee this year—sixty years—you know."

"H'm," said the old lady. "Sixty. George III reigned sixty-three. But they all go in time. I remember my dear father coming up to my nursery after the funeral of poor young Edward VI. He was one of the Court pages, you know—that is, when Henry VIII was King. Such a handsome lad—there is his portrait . . . somewhere."

For a moment Alice's mind was a whirlpool of vague memories—memories of what she had read in her history-books.

But Miss Cheyney's bead-like notes had hardly paused. "You must understand that I have not asked you to come this long way by one of those horrid new-fangled steam-engines just to gossip about my childhood. Kings and Queens come and go like the rest of things. And though I have seen many changes, it seems to me the world is pretty much the same as ever. Nor can I believe that the newspaper is a beneficial novelty. When I was a girl we managed well enough without, and even in Mr. Addison's day one small sheet twice a week was enough. But there, complaint is useless. And you cannot exactly be held responsible for all that. There were changes in my girlhood, too—great changes. The world was not so crowded then. There was nobility and beauty. Yes." Her eyes wandered, to rest a moment on the portrait of the young woman in the primrose gown. "The truth is, my dear," she continued, "I have to tell you something, and I wish you to listen."

Once more she remained silent a moment, clutching the handkerchief she held between her fingers. "What I desire you to tell *me*," she said at last, leaning stealthily forward in her great chair, "what I am anxious that you should tell me is, How long do you wish to live?"

For a few moments Alice sat cold and motionless. It was as if an icy breath straight from the North Pole had swept across the room, congealing with its horror the very air. Her eyes wandered vacantly from picture to picture, from ancient object to ancient object—aged, mute and lifeless—to rest at last on a flowering weed that reared its head beyond one of the diamond-shaped panes of glass in the window.

"I have never thought of that, great-grandmamma," her dry lips whispered. "I don't think I know."

"Well, I am not expecting an old head on young shoulders," retorted the old lady. "Perhaps if King Charles had realized that—so learned, so generous, so faithful a monarch—I doubt if that vulgar creature Oliver Cromwell would ever have succeeded in having his off."

The acorn head drew down into its laces like a snail into its shell. Until this moment Alice might have been conversing with an exquisite image, or an automaton—the glittering eyes, the crooked fingers, the voice from afar. But now it seemed life itself was stirring in it. The tiny yet piercing tones sank almost to a whisper, the head stirred furtively from side to side as if to be sure no eavesdropper were within earshot.

"Now listen close to me, my child: I have a secret. A secret which I wish to share only with you. You would suppose, wouldn't you, that this being the three-hundred-and-fiftieth anniversary of my natal day"—and at this the dreadful realization suddenly swept over

Alice that she had quite forgotten to wish her godmother "Many happy returns"—"you might suppose that you are about to meet a gay and numerous company here—young and happy creatures like yourself. But no: not so. Even your dear mother is, of course, only my great-great-great-great-great-great-great-granddaughter-*in-law*. She was a Miss Wilmot, I believe."

"Yes, Woodcot, great-grandmamma," said Alice softly.

"Well, Woodcot," said the old lady; "it is no matter. It is you, my child, whom I have made, to be precise, my chosen. In mere men I take no interest. Not only that, but you must now be of the age I was when the portrait you see on yonder wall was painted. It is the work of a pupil of Hans Holbein's. Hans Holbein himself, I believe, was dead at the time. Dear me, child, I remember sitting for that portrait in this very room—as if it were yesterday. It was much admired by Sir Walter Raleigh, who, you may remember, came to so unhappy an end. That was, I recollect, in my early seventies. My father and his father were boys together in Devonshire."

Alice blinked a little—she could not turn her eyes away from her godmother's—that mammet-like face, those minute motionless hands.

"Now glance at that picture, please!" the old lady bade her, pointing a tiny crooked-up forefinger towards the further wall. "Do you see any resemblance?"

Alice looked long and steadily at the portrait. But she had neither the courage nor vanity to deny that the fair smiling features were at least a *little* like her own. "To whom, great-grandmamma?" Alice whispered.

"'To whom?' Well, well, well!" came the reply, the words sounding like the chiming of a distant silver bell.

"I see it. I see it. . . . But never mind that now. Did you perhaps look at this *house* as you made your way up the avenue?"

"Oh yes, great-grandmamma—though I couldn't, of course, look close, you know," Alice managed to say.

"Did you *enjoy* its appearance?"

"I don't think I thought of that," said Alice. "The trees and park were very lovely. I have never seen such —*mature* trees, great-grandmamma. And yet all their leaves were budding and some were fully out. Isn't it wonderful for trees so—so long in the world to—why, to come out at all?"

"I was referring to the house," said the old lady. "*Springs* nowadays are not what they used to be. They have vanished from the England I once knew. I remember once an April when angels were seen on the hilltops above London. But that is no matter for us now: not now. The house?"

Once again Alice's gaze wandered—to come to rest again on the green, nodding weed at the window.

"It is a very very quiet house," she said.

The childlike tones died between the thick stone walls; and a profound silence followed them, like that of water in a well. Meanwhile, as Alice fully realized, her godmother had been fixedly searching her face with her remote but intent eyes. It was as if Time itself were only a child and that of this aged face he had made his little secret gazebo.

"Now please listen to me very carefully," she continued at last. "Such a countenance as yours—one bearing the least resemblance to that portrait over there, must be the possessor of a fair share of wits. I am old enough, my child, not to be charged, I hope, with the folly of vanity. In my girlhood I enjoyed a due share of admiration. And I have a proposal to make to you which will need all the sagacity you are capable of. Don't be alarmed. I have every faith in you. But first, I want you to go into the next room, where you will find a meal prepared. Young people nowadays, I hear, need continuous nourishment. What wonder! Since they have forgotten all the manners of a lady as *I* know them, and are never still for a moment together. What wonder! With all these dreadful machines I hear of, the discontent, the ignorance and folly, the noise and unrest and confusion. In my young days the poor were the poor and the humble the humble, my child; and knew their place. In my young days I would sit contented for hours at a time over a simple piece of embroidery. And if I needed it, my mother never deigned to spare the rod. But there, I didn't invite you to visit an old woman merely to listen to a sermon. When you have refreshed yourself you are to take a little walk through the house. Go wherever you please; look well about you; no one will disturb you. And in an hour's time come back to me here again. Nowadays I take a little sleep in the afternoon. I shall be ready for you then. . . ."

Alice, with a relief beyond words, rose from her chair. She curtsied again towards the small, motionless figure in the distance, and retired through the dark oak door.

The room in which she at once found herself was small, hexagonal, and panelled with the blackest of old oak. A copper candelabrum hung from the dark moulded ceiling, and beyond the leaded panes she could see the gigantic trees in the park. To her dismay the footman who had accompanied the butler into the room when her god-mother had first made her appearance, was stationed behind the chair at the table. Never had Alice supposed that it was proper for men-servants, except perhaps gardeners, to wear long grey beards. But there he was, with his dim sidling eyes. And she must needs turn her back on him to seat herself at the table. She nibbled the fruit and bread, the rich cake and the sweetmeats which he presented in their heavy silver dishes, and she sipped her sweet drink. But it was a hasty and nervous meal, and she tasted nothing of what she had eaten.

As soon as it was over, the servant opened the door for her, and she began her voyage of discovery through the great, deserted house. It was as if her very ghost were her only company. Never had solitude so oppressed her, never before had she been so intensely aware of being wideawake and yet dreaming. The long corridors, the low and crooked lintelled doors, the dark uneven floors, their Persian mats, their tapestries and hangings, only the lovelier in that their colours had been dimmed by so many suns, the angled flights of stairs, the solemn air that brooded between the walls, the multitude of pictures, the huge beds, the endless succession of superannuated coffers, daybeds, cabinets—all this in but a few minutes had tired and fatigued Alice far more even than the long journey from the home of her childhood that morning. Upstairs and downstairs, on she wandered for all the world like the goosey-goosey-gander of the old nursery rhyme.

And when at last with a sigh she glanced at the bright little silver watch which had been her mother's birthday gift, its slender hands told her that she had s ill a full quarter-of-an-hour before she need return to her great-great-great-great-great-great-great-great-grandmother's room.

That in which she had now found herself seemed to be a small library. Its walls were ranged from ceiling to floor with old leather and lambskin folios and quartos and squat duodecimos, while between them hung portraits and the loveliest miniatures and medallions of scores upon scores of persons whom she guessed must be her ancestors and ancestresses of goodness knows how many monarchs ago.

One or two of the pictures, indeed, as the crabbed inscriptions showed, had been gifts to the family from those monarchs themselves. In their various costumes, wigs, turbans and furbelows they looked as if they must have been the guests at an immense fancy-dress ball.

What tho Felicitie befal?
Time makyth shadowes of us all.

In this room a low recess filled the shallow bow window and on this lay a strip of tapestry. The leaded pane of the window was open. The sun was already westering, its beams slanting in on the gilt and ebony and ivory of the frames suspended from their nails. Alice knelt down at the window; and her mind slipped into a day-dream, and her gaze wandered far away over the golden budding tops of the enormous oaks, the flat dark outstretched motionless palms of the cedars—perhaps descendants of those which Sir Philip Sidney had brought home to his beloved England from the East.

The thoughts that had all day been skittering in her mind like midges over a pool, gradually fell still, and she sank deeper and deeper into the hush that lay over the ancient house. It was as if its walls were those of an enormous diving-bell sunken beyond measure in an unfathomable ocean of Time. So tranquil was the sweet April air beyond the window that she could actually detect the sound of the browsing of the herd of fallow deer that had now closely approached the lawns of the house itself.

And as, lost in this reverie she sat entranced, she became conscious that a small living animal—the like of which she had never seen before—had crept up within a pace or two of her on the window-sill, and was now steadily regarding her with its clear bead-brown eyes. In size it was rather larger than a mole, its dark thick fur was soft as a beaver's, and it had a short, furry, and tufted tail. Its ears were cocked on its head, its silvery whiskers turned downwards above its jaws, and Alice could see its tiny ivory claws as it sat there erect on its haunches like a tame cat or a dog begging for a titbit of meat. Alice, alas, had nothing to offer her visitor, not even a cherry-stone, not even a crumb.

"Well, you pretty thing," she whispered, "what is it?"

The creature's whiskers moved ever so slightly, its eyes fixed more intently than ever on the face of this strange visitor. Very very delicately Alice thrust out her finger, and to her astonishment found herself gently caressing the furry nose. "It was as if I was in Wonderland, myself," she explained long afterwards to her mother. Perfectly mute and still, the owner of it seemed to enjoy this little courtesy. And when she had withdrawn her finger, it looked at her more closely and searchingly than ever, as if bidding her take heed. It then tapped repeatedly with its ivory-clawed paw on the oak casement, glanced searchingly at her yet again, then shook its furry head vehemently three times, paused, turned swiftly about and pattered away into hiding behind a huge carved Moorish cabinet before Alice could so much as bid it adieu.

Quiet little events in this life, even though we cannot understand what exactly they mean, are apt to *seem* to mean a great deal. So with this small animal and Alice. It was as if—though she was not aware of it—she had been brooding over a problem in Algebra or a proposition in Euclid, and it had ventured out of its living-place to tell her the answer. How fantastic a notion!—when Alice knew neither the problem nor what its solution was.

She glanced at her watch once more; her fair cheeks pinking all over at realizing that she was now ten minutes late for her assignation with her godmother.

She must be gone. None the less, she had time to look her farewell at the huge dreaming park before she set out on her return journey.

Before at last finding her way, however, she irretrievably lost it. For the house was a silent maze of deceptive passages and corridors. Every fresh attempt only increased her confusion, and then suddenly she found herself looking into a room utterly different from any she had yet seen. Its low walls were of stone, its dusty windows shuttered; it contained nothing but a chair. And in that chair sat what appeared to be the life-size image of the smiling lovely creature she had seen in the portrait—eyes shut, cheeks a faint rose, hair still shimmering with gold, its hands laid idly in the lap, the fingers of one of them clutching what seemed to be the dried-up fragments of a bunch of roses. What there was to alarm her in this harmless image she could not tell; but she gazed awhile at it in horror, closed-to the door and ran off as if pursued by a nightmare, down one corridor and up another, to find herself at last by good fortune once more in the room where she had had her meal. It seemed, as she stood there, her hand upon her breast, as if she would never again recover her breath. She was no longer nervous; no longer merely timid: she was afraid. "If only, if only I had never come to this house!" was her one terrified thought.

She discovered with relief on re-entering Miss Cheyney's presence that her godmother was still asleep. Alice could see awhile without being seen.

Now one of her mother's brothers—one of Alice's uncles, that is—was an old bachelor who delighted in birthday gifts. Alice had therefore been richer in dolls than most children: wooden, wax, china, Dutch,

French, Russian, and even one from the Andaman Islands. But no single one of them had shown a face so utterly still and placid as that now leaning gently aside in its lace and silver cap and mantle. There was no expression whatever on its features. No faintest smile; no shadow of a frown. And yet, the tiny wrinkles all over it, crooking down even from the brows over the eyelids, gave it the appearance of an exquisitely figured map.

And Alice was still surveying it as closely as some old treasure-hunter might the chart of his secret island, when the minute eyes reopened and her godmother was instantly awake and intent.

"Ah," whispered she, "I have myself been on a long journey, but I heard you calling. What happens, I wonder," and the tones sank lower, "what happens when one has ventured on too far to hear any such rumours. Answer me that, eh? But no matter. There is a more important question first. Tell me now, if you please, what you think of my house."

Alice moistened her lips. "That, great-grandmamma," she managed to reply at last, "that would take *ages*. It is marvellous: but oh, so very still."

"What should there be to disturb it?" asked the old lady.

Alice shook her head.

"Tell me," and her voice tinkled across the air with a peculiar little tang, "would you like this house for your own?"

"This House—for my own?" breathed the young girl.

"Ay, for your own, and for always—humanly speaking."

"I don't quite understand," said Alice.

The little head leaned sidelong like an inquisitive bird's.

"Naturally, my child. You *cannot* until I have gone a little further. The gift I am now offering you is one that few human beings in this world conceive to be possible. It is not merely this house, my child, with all that it contains—much as that may be. It is life. My father, you must understand, was a traveller; and in days when danger was a man's constant companion. In this very room on his return from a many years' journey, he told me as a girl of a dismal mountainous region of snow and ice and precipices that lies *there*—West of China, I believe. It was from thence that he brought back his secret. It was one that for grievous and tragical reasons he could not follow himself. And I, my child, was his only choice. You will realize there may come a day when the wish to live on may have somewhat dimmed in my mind. I confess to feeling a little weariness at times. But before I go, it is my privilege—my obligation—to confer the secret on another. Look at me:" the voice rose a little; it was as though a wren had uttered its shrill song in the low resounding room. "I am offering this inestimable benefit to *you*."

Alice sat straight as a dart in her chair, not venturing to turn her eyes aside even for a moment.

"The secret, great-grandmamma?"

"Ay," continued the old woman, closing her eyes, "you heard me aright. I will presently whisper it into your ear. Imagine, my child, the wonder of infinite time! Imagine a life in such surroundings as these, far from all the follies and vexations of the world—and one fear—the most terrible of all fears—gone, or at any rate so remote as to be of no consequence. Imagine that, I say."

For an instant Alice's gaze wavered. Her eyes glanced swiftly towards the window where shone the swiftly changing colours of the sunset; where sang the wild birds, and Spring was fleeting on her way.

"Take your own time: and do not be afraid of me. I shall make few conditions. Only that you must vow silence, to breathe not one syllable of what I shall tell you—not even to your own mother. All else will be easy—comparatively easy. All else. You will come here and live with me. Rooms are prepared for you—books, music, horses to ride, servants to wait on you, all that you need. And in due season this house, this accumulation of things precious and old and beautiful, this wide park stretching for many more miles than you can see from my topmost windows, will be yours alone. You may pine for a while for old friends. It is an unhappy thing to say good-bye, as I have heard. But all fades, all goes. And in time you will not wish for company. Servants as aged as mine are not difficult to find; they are discreet, and have need to remain faithful. We shall have many a quiet talk together. I have much to tell you. I long, my dear child, to share memories with you that I have never breathed to a living soul. There are wings to this house into which you cannot have penetrated, simply because they are shut off by bolts and bars. They contain much to see: much to linger over; much to wonder at. Yes, and my dear child, in you I should live on—our two minds . . . two lives. Tell me now, what do you think of my proposal? And remember this:—Not even Solomon in all his glory could have conferred on you what I now offer."

The aged head was nodding—as if with fatigue. The cramped fingers fumbled aimlessly with the lace handkerchief, and Alice's poor wits were once more in a desperate confusion. The room swam dizzily before her eyes. She shut them a moment; endeavouring in vain to consider calmly what that remote unhuman voice had been saying to her. She might as well have struggled in sleep to shake off the veils and nets of a dream, the snares of a nightmare. One thing only was audible to her now, a bird singing in the garden and the sound of her shoe tapping on the floor. She listened —and came back.

"You mean," she whispered, "on and on and on—like you, great-grandmamma?"

The old lady made no reply.

"May I, do you think, then, if you would be so kind, may I have time to think it over?"

"Think what over?" said her godmother. "Are you supposing a child of your age can think over three complete centuries before a single moment of them has come into view?"

"No," said Alice, her courage returning a little, "I meant, think over what you have said. It is so very difficult to realize what it means."

"It means," said the old lady, "an immeasurable sea, infinite space, an endless vista—of time. It means freedom from the cares and anxieties and follies that are the lot of the poor creatures in the world beyond—living out their few days in brutish stupidity. You are still young, but who knows? It means, my child, postponing a visit to a certain old friend of ours—whose name is Death."

She breathed the word as if in begrudged pleasure at its sound. Alice shuddered, and yet it gave her fresh resolution. She rose from her chair.

"I am young and stupid, I know, great-grandmamma; and I would do anything in the world not to—not to hurt your feelings. And of course, of course I know that most people have a very hard time and that most of us are not very sharp-witted. But you said *death*; and I think, if you will forgive my saying so, I would rather I should have to die when—just when, I mean, I *must* die. You see, it would be a very sorrowful thing for me if it came after my mother had—if, I mean, she cannot share the secret too? And even then. . . . Why cannot we all share it? I do see, indeed I do, there is very little time in this world in which to grow wise. But when you think of the men who have——"

"You are here, my child," Miss Cheyney interrupted her, "to answer questions—not to ask them. I must not be fatigued. Then I should have no sleep. But surely you are old enough to know that there is not a human creature in a thousand, nay, not one in a hundred thousand, who has any hope of growing wise, not if he lived till Doomsday."

She edged forward an inch in her chair. "Suppose, my child, your refusal means that this secret will perish with—with *me?* Unless," the voice sank to a muttering, "unless *you* consent to share it? Eh, what then?"

Alice found her eyes fixed on the old lady like a bird's on a serpent, and the only answer she could make was a violent shake of the head. "Oh," she cried, suddenly bursting into tears, "I simply can't tell you how grateful I am for all your kindness, and how miserable I seem to myself to be saying this. But please, Miss Cheyney, may I go now? I feel a dreadful thing might happen if I stay here a minute longer."

The old lady seemed to be struggling in her chair, as if in the effort to rise out of it; but her strength failed her. She lifted her claw-like mittened hand into the air.

"Begone at once, then," she whispered, "at once. Even my patience is limited. And when the day comes that will remind you of my kindness, may you wish you had . . . Oh, oh! . . ." The frail voice rose shrill as a gnat's, then ceased. At sound of it the old butler came hastening in at the further door; and Alice slipped out of the other. . . .

Not until the house had vanished from sight behind the leaping branches of its forest-trees did she slacken her pace to recover her breath. She had run wildly on, not daring to pause or even glance over her shoulder, as if her guardian angel were at her heels, lending wings to her feet to save her from danger.

That evening she and her mother—seated in the cosy red-curtained coffee-room of the "Red Lion" actually sipped together a brimming glass of the landlord's old Madeira. Alice had never before kept any secret from her mother. Yet though she was able to tell her most of what had happened that afternoon, she could not persuade herself to utter a syllable about the purpose which had prompted Miss Cheyney to send her so improbable an invitation. Not then, nor ever afterwards.

"Do you really mean, my own dearest," her mother repeated more than once, pressing her hand as they sat in the chill spring night under the old oil lamp-post awaiting their train in the little country railway station; "do you mean she never gave you a single little keepsake; never offered you *anything* out of all those wonderful treasures in that dreadful old house?"

"She asked me, mother dear," said Alice, turning her face away towards the dark-mouthed tunnel through which they would soon be venturing—"she asked me if I would like ever to be as old as she was. And honestly, I said I would much prefer to stay just the silly green creature I am, so long as I can be with you."

It was an odd thing to do—if the station-master had been watching them—but, however odd, it is certainly true that at this moment mother and daughter turned and flung their arms about each other's necks and kissed each other in such a transport as if they had met again for the first time after an enormous journey.

Not that Alice had been quite accurate in saying that her godmother had made her no gift. For a day or two afterwards there came by post a package; and enwrapped in its folds of old Chinese paper Alice found the very portrait she had seen on the wall on that already seemingly far-off day—the drawing, I mean, made by a pupil of the famous Hans Holbein, depicting her great-great-great-great-great-great-great-great-grandmother in the year of grace 1564, when she was just turned seventeen.

A Penny a Day

Once upon a time, there lived in a cottage that had been built out of the stones of a ruinous Castle and stood within its very walls, an old woman, and her grand-daughter—whose name was Griselda. Here they lived quite alone, being the only two left of a family of farmers who had once owned a wide track of land around them—fields, meadows, heath and moorland—skirting the cliffs and the sea.

But all this was long ago. Now Griselda and her old grandmother had little left but the roof over their heads and a long garden whose apples and cherries and plum-trees flowered in spring under the very walls of the Castle. Many birds nested in this quiet hollow; and the murmur of the sea on the beach beyond it was never hushed to rest.

The old woman tended the garden. And Griselda had very little time wherein to be idle. After her day's work in the farms and fields, she went so weary to bed that however much she tried to keep awake in order to enjoy the company of her own thoughts, she was usually fast asleep before the wick of her tallow candle had ceased to smoulder. Yet for reasons not known even to herself she was as happy as she was beautiful. In looks she resembled a mermaid. Her fair face was unusually gentle and solemn, which may in part have come from her love and delight in gazing at and listening to the sea.

Whenever she had time to herself, which was very seldom, she would climb up by the broken weed-grown steps to the very top of the Castle tower, and sit there —like Fatima's sister—looking out over the green cliffs and the vast flat blue of the ocean. She sat as small as a manikin there. When the sea-winds had blown themselves out she would search the beach for driftwood—the only human creature to be seen—in the thin salt spray blown in on the wind. And the sea-birds would scream around her while the slow toppling Atlantic breakers shook the earth with their thunder. In still evenings, too, when storms had been raging far out over the ocean, and only a slow ground-swell poured in its heavy waters on the shore, it seemed that sunken bells were ringing from a belfry submerged and hidden for ever in the deeps.

But no humans, except Griselda, were there to listen. It was seldom, even, that the people in the nearest village came down to the sea-strand; and never when night was falling. For the Castle was a place forbidden. It was the haunt, it was said, of the Strange Folk. On calm summer evenings unearthly dancers had been seen dancing between the dusk and the moonlight on the short green turf at the verge of the sands, where bugloss and sea-lavender bloomed, and the gulls had their meeting place, gabbling softly together as they preened their wings in the twilight.

Griselda had often heard these tales. But, as she had lived under the walls of the Castle, and had played alone in its ruins ever since she could remember anything at all, she listened to them with delight. What was there to be afraid of? She longed to see these dancers; and kept watch. And when the full moon was ablaze in the sky, she would slip out of her grandmother's

cottage and dance alone in its dazzling light on the hard, sea-laid sands of the beach; or sit, half-dreaming, in some green knoll of the cliffs. She would listen to the voices of the sea among the rocks and in the caves; and could not believe that what she heard was only the lully and music of its waters.

Often, too, when sitting on her sun-warmed door-step, morning or evening, mending her clothes, or peeling potatoes, or shelling peas, or scouring out some old copper pot, she would feel, all in an instant, that she was no longer alone. Then she would stoop her head a little lower over her needle or basin, pretending not to notice that anything was different. As you can hear the notes of an unseen bird or in the darkness can smell a flower past the finding, so it was with Griselda. She had company beyond hearing, touch, or sight.

Now and again, too, as she slid her downcast eyes to right or left, she had actually caught a fleeting glimpse of a shape, not *quite* real perhaps, but more real than nothing—though it might be half-hidden behind the bushes, or peering down at her from an ivy-shadowed hollow in the thick stone walls.

Such things did not alarm Griselda—no more than would the wind in the keyhole, or the cry of flighting swans at night. They were part of her life, just as the rarer birds and beetles and moths and butterflies are part of the Earth's life. And whatever these shadowy creatures were, she was certain they meant her no harm.

So the happy days went by, spring on to winter, though Griselda had to work nearly all her waking hours to keep herself and her old grandmother from want. Then, one day, the old woman fell ill. She had fallen on the narrow stairs as she was shuffling down in the morning, and there, at the foot of them, looking no more alive than a bundle of old clothes, Griselda found her when she came in with her driftwood.

She was old, and worn and weary, and Griselda knew well that unless great care was taken of her, she might get worse; and even die. The thought of this terrified her. "Oh, Grannie, Grannie!" she kept whispering to herself as she went about her work, "I'll do anything—anything in the world—I don't mind what happens—if only you'll promise not to *die*!" But she soon began to take courage again, and kept such a cheerful face that the old woman hadn't an inkling of how sick with care and foreboding Griselda's small head often was, or how near her heart came to despair.

She scarcely had time now to wash her face or comb her hair, or even to sleep and eat. She seldom sat down to a meal, and even when she did, there was but a minute or two in which to gobble it up. She was so tired she could scarcely drag her feet up the steep narrow staircase; the colour began to fade out of her cheeks, and her face to grow haggard and wan.

Still, she toiled on, still sang over her work, and simply refused to be miserable. And however sick and hungry and anxious she might feel, she never let her grandmother see that she was. The old soul lay helpless and in pain on her bed, and had troubles enough of her own. So Griselda had nobody to share hers with; and instead of their getting better they grew worse.

And when—after a hot breathless night during which she had lain between waking and dreaming while the lightning flared at her window, and the thunder raved over the sea—when, next morning she came down very early to find that the hungry mice had stolen more than half of the handful of oatmeal she had left in the cupboard, and that her little crock of milk had turned sour, her heart all but failed her. She sat down on the doorstep and she began to cry.

It was early in May; the flashing dark blue sea was tumbling among the rocks of the beach, its surf like snow. The sun blazed in the east, and all around her the trees in their new leaves were blossoming, and the birds singing, and the air was cool and fragrant with flowers after the rain.

In a little while Griselda stopped crying—and very few tears had trickled down from her eyes—and with her chin propped on her hands, she sat staring out across the bright green grass, her eyes fixed vacantly on three butterflies that were chasing one another in the calm sweet air. This way, that way, they glided, fluttered, dipped and soared; then suddenly swooped up into the dazzling blue of the sky above the high broken wall and vanished from sight.

Griselda sighed. It was as if they had been mocking her misery. And with that sigh, there was no more breath left in her body. So she had to take a much deeper breath to make up for it. After that she sighed no more—since she had suddenly become aware again that she was being watched. And this time she knew by what. Not twelve paces away, at the top of a flight of tumble-down stone steps that corkscrewed up to one of the Castle turrets, stood what seemed to be an old wizened pygmy hunched-up old man.

He was of the height of a child of five; he had pointed ears, narrow shoulders, and a hump on his back. And he wore a coat made of a patchwork of moleskins. He stood there—as stock-still as the stones themselves—his bright colourless eyes under his moleskin cap fixed on her, as if Griselda was as outlandish an object to him as he was to Griselda.

She shut her own for a moment, supposing he might have come out of her fancy; then looked again. But already his crook'd staff in his hand, the dwarf had come rapidly shuffling along over the turf towards her. And yet again he stayed—a few paces away. Then, fixing his small bright gaze on her face, he asked her in a shrill, cracked, rusty voice why she was crying. In spite of their lightness, his eyes were piercingly sharp in his dried-up face. And Griselda, as she watched him, marvelled how any living creature could look so old.

Gnarled, wind-shorn trees—hawthorn and scrub oak—grew here and there in the moorland above the sea, and had stood there for centuries among the yellow gorse and sea-pinks. He looked older even than these. She told him she had nothing to cry about, except only that the mice had been at her oatmeal, the milk had turned sour, and she didn't know where to turn next. He asked her what she had to do, and she told him that too.

At this he crinkled up his pin-sharp eyes, as if he were thinking, and glanced back at the turret from which he had come. Then, as if he had made up his mind, he shuffled a step or two nearer and asked Griselda what wages she would pay him if he worked for her for nine days. "For three days, and three days, and three days," he said, "and that's all. How much?"

Griselda all but laughed out loud at this. She told the dwarf that far from being able to pay anyone to work for her, there wasn't a farthing in the house—and not even food enough to offer him a taste of breakfast. "Unless", she said, "you would care for a cold potato. There's one or two of *them* left over from supper."

"Ay, nay, nay," said the dwarf. "I won't work without wages, and I can get my own food. But hark now: if you'll promise to give me a penny a day for nine days, I will work here for you from dawn to dark. Then you yourself will be able to be off to the farms and the fields. But it must be a penny a day and no less; it must be paid every evening at sunset before I go to my own parts again; and the old woman up there must never see me, and shall hardly know that I have come."

Griselda sat looking at him—as softly and easily as she could; but she had never in all her days seen any human being like this before. Though his face was wizened and cockled up like a winter apple, yet it seemed as if he could never have been any different. He looked as old as the stones around him and yet no older than the snapdragons that grew in them. To meet his eyes was like peering through a rusty keyhole into a long empty room. She expected at any instant he would vanish away, or be changed into something utterly different—a flowering thistle or a heap of stones!

Long before this very morning, indeed, Griselda had often caught sight of what looked like living shapes and creatures—on the moorland or the beach—which, when she had looked again, were clean gone; or, when she had come close, proved to be only a furze-bush, or a rock jutting out of the turf, or a scangle of sheep's

wool caught on a thorn. This is the way of these strangers. While then she was not in the least afraid of the dwarf, she felt uneasy and bewildered in his company.

But she continued to smile at him, and answered that though she could not promise to pay him a penny until she had a penny to pay, she would do her best to earn some. Now nothing was left. And she had already made up her mind to be off at once to a farm along the sea-cliffs, where she would be almost sure to get work. If the dwarf would wait but one day, she told him, she would ask the farmer to pay her her wages before she came home again. "Then I *could* give you the penny," she said.

Old Moleskins continued to blink at her. "Well," he said, "be off then now. And be back before sunset."

But first Griselda made her grandmother a bowl of water-porridge, using up for it the last pinch of meal she had in the house. This she carried up to the old woman, with a sprig of apple blossom in a gallipot to put beside it and make it taste better. Since she had so promised him, and felt sure he meant no harm, she said nothing to her grandmother about the dwarf. She tidied the room, tucked in the bedclothes, gave the old woman some water to wash in, beat up her pillow, pinned a shawl over her shoulders, and, having made her as comfortable as she could manage, and left her to herself, promising to be home again as soon as she could.

"And be sure, Grannie," she said, "whatever happens, not to stir from your bed."

By good fortune, the farmer's wife whom she went off to see along the sea-cliffs was making butter that morning. The farmer knew Griselda well, and when she had finished helping his wife and the dairymaid with the churning, he not only paid her two pennies for her pains, but a third, "For the sake", as he said, "of your goldilocks, my dear; and *they*'re worth a king's ransom! . . . What say you, Si?" he called to his son, who had just come in with the calves. Simon, his face all red, and he was a good deal uglier (though pleasant in face) than his father, glanced up at Griselda, but the gold must have dazzled his eyes, for he turned away and said nothing.

At this moment the farmer's wife came bustling out into the yard again. She had brought Griselda not only a pitcher of new milk and a couple of hen's eggs to take to her grandmother, but some lardy-cakes and a jar of honey for herself. So Griselda, feeling ten times happier than she had been for many a long day, hurried off home.

Now there was a duck-pond under a willow on the way she took home, and there, remembering what the farmer had said, she paused, stooped over, and looked at herself in the muddy water. But the sky was of the brightest blue above her head; and there were so many smooth oily ripples on the surface of the water made by the ducks as they swam and preened and gossiped together that Griselda couldn't see herself clearly, or be sure from its reflection even if her hair was still gold! She got up, laughed to herself, waved her hand to the ducks and hastened on.

When, carrying her pitcher, she had come in under the high snapdragon-tufted gateway of the Castle, and so home again, a marvel it was to see. The kitchen was as neat as a new pin. The table had been scoured; the fire-irons twinkled like silver; the crockery on the dresser looked as if it had been newly painted; a brown jar of wallflowers bloomed sweet on the sill, and even the brass pendulum of the cuckoo-clock, that hadn't ticked for years, shone round as the sun at noonday, and was swinging away as if it meant to catch up before nightfall all the time it had ever lost.

Beside the hearth, too, lay a pile of broken driftwood, a fire was merrily dancing in the grate, there was a fish cooking in the pan in the brick oven, the old iron kettle hung singing from its hook; and a great saucepan, brimful of peeled potatoes, sat in the hearth beneath it to keep it company. And not only this, for there lay on the table a dish of fresh-pulled salad—lettuces, radishes, and young sorrel and dandelion leaves. But of Old Moleskins, not a sign.

Griselda herself was a good housewife, but in all her

days she had never seen the kitchen look like this. It was as fresh as a daisy. And Griselda began to sing—to keep the kettle company. Having made a custard out of one of the eggs and the milk she had brought home with her, she climbed upstairs again to see her grandmother.

"Well, Grannie," she said, "how are you now? I've been away and come back. I haven't wasted a moment; but you must be nearly starving."

The old woman told her she had spent the morning between dozing and dreaming and looking from her bed out of the window at the sea. For by good luck exactly opposite her bedroom window was the broken opening of what once was a window in the walls of the Castle. It was a kind of spy-hole into the world for the old woman.

"And what else were you going to tell me, Grannie?" said Griselda.

The old woman spied about her from her pillow as if she were afraid she might be overheard. Then she warned Griselda that next time she went out she must make sure to latch the door. Some strange animal must have been prowling about in the house, she said. She had heard it not only under her open window, but even stirring about in the room below. "Though I must say," she added, "I had to listen pretty hard!"

Griselda glanced up out of the lattice window and, since her head was a good deal higher than her grandmother's pillow, she could see down into the green courtyard below. And there stood Old Moleskins, looking up at her.

An hour or two afterwards, when the sun was dipping behind the green hills beyond the village, and Griselda sat alone, beside the fire, her sewing in her lap, she heard shuffling footsteps on the cobbles outside, and the dwarf appeared at the window. Griselda thanked him with all her heart for what he had done for her, and took out of her grandmother's old leather purse one of the three pennies she had earned at the farm.

The dwarf eyed it greedily, then, pointing with his thumb at an old pewter pot that stood on the chimney-shelf, told Griselda to put the penny in it and to keep it safe for him until he asked for it.

"Nine days", he said, "I will work for you—three and three and three—and no more, for the same wages. And then you must pay me all you owe me. And I will come every evening to see it into the pot."

So Griselda, tiptoe on the kitchen fender, put the penny in the pot, and shut down the lid. When she turned round again Old Moleskins was gone.

Before she went to bed that night, she peeped out of the door. There was no colour left in the sky except the dark blue of night; but a slip of moon, as thin as copper wire, hung in the west above the hill, and would soon be following the sun beyond it. Griselda solemnly bowed to the moon seven times, and shook the old purse in her pocket.

When she came down the next morning, the kitchen had been swept, a fire was dancing up the chimney, her mug and plate and spoon had been laid on the table, and a smoking bowl of milk-porridge was warming itself on the hearth. When Griselda took the porridge up to her grandmother, the old woman gazed at her in astonishment, for Griselda had been but a minute gone. She took a sip of the porridge, smacked her lips, tasted it again, and asked Griselda what she had put in it to flavour it. It was a taste she had never tasted before. And Griselda told the old woman it was a secret.

That day the farmer gave Griselda some old gold-brown Cochin-China hens to pluck for market. "They've seen better days, but will do for the pot," he said. And having heard that her grandmother was better, he kept her working for him till late in the afternoon. So Griselda plucked and singed busily on, grieved for the old hens, but happy to think of her wages. Then once more the farmer paid her her twopence; and, once more, a penny over; this time not for the sake of her bright gold hair, but for her "glass-grey eyes". So now there was fivepence in her purse, and as yet there had been no need, beyond last night's penny for the dwarf, to spend any of them.

When Griselda came home, not only was everything in the kitchen polished up brighter than ever, but a pot of broth was simmering on the hob, which, to judge by the savour of it, contained not only carrots and onions and pot-herbs but a young rabbit. Besides which, a strip of the garden had been freshly dug; three rows of brisk young cabbages had been planted, and what Griselda guessed was two more of broad beans and peas. Whatever the dwarf had set his hand to was a job well done.

Sharp to his time—the sun had but that very moment dipped beneath the hills—he came to the kitchen door for his wages. Griselda smiled at him, thanked him, and took out a penny. He gazed at it earnestly; then at her. And he said, "Put that in the pot, too." So now there were two pennies in his pewter pot and four pennies in Griselda's purse.

And so the days went by. Her grandmother grew steadily better, and on the next Sunday—muffled up in a shawl like an old tortoiseshell cat—she sat up a little while beside her window. On most mornings Griselda had gone out to work at the farm or in the village; on one or two she had stayed in the house and sat with her grandmother to finish her sewing and mending or any other work she had found to do.

While she was in the cottage she never saw the dwarf, though he might be hidden away in the garden. But still her grandmother talked of the strange stirrings and noises she heard when Griselda was away. "You'd have thought", the old woman said, "there was a whole litter of young pigs in the kitchen, and the old sow, too!"

On the eighth day, the farmer not only gave Griselda her tuppence for her wages and another for the sake of "the dimple in her cheek," but the third penny had a hole in it. "And that's for luck," said the farmer. She went home rejoicing. And seeing no reason why she shouldn't share her luck with the dwarf, she put the penny with the hole in it into the pewter pot when he came that evening. And as usual he said not a word. He merely watched Griselda's face with his colourless eyes while she thanked him for what he had done, and then watched her put his penny into the pot. Then in an instant he was gone.

"That maid Griselda, from the Castle yonder," said the farmer to his wife that night as, candlestick in hand, the two of them were going up to bed, "she seems to me as willing as she's neat and pretty. And if she takes as good care of the pence as she seems to, my dear, there's never a doubt, I warrant, but as she will take as good care of the pounds!"

And he was right. Griselda had taken such good care of the pence that at this very moment she was sitting alone in the kitchen in the light of her solitary candle and slowly putting down on paper every penny that she had paid and every penny that she had spent:

Acounts

receeved		Spent	
from Farmer for wages	10	oatmeel	2
prezants	5	bones for soop	2
wages from Missus Jakes	2	shuger	2
wages for piggs	1	hair ribon	1
	—	wole	1
	18	doll	1
		money for Moalskins	8
			—
			17

The doll had been a present for the cowman's little daughter. And though Griselda had made many mistakes before she got her sum right, it was right *now*; and here was the penny over in her purse to prove it.

The next evening, a little before sunset, Griselda sat waiting for the dwarf to come. Never had she felt so happy and light-hearted. It was the last of his nine days; she had all his nine pennies ready for him—one in her purse and eight in the pewter pot; the farmer had promised her as much work as she could manage; her old grandmother was nearly well again; the cupboard was no longer bare; and she was thankful beyond all words. It seemed as if her body could not possibly contain her happiness.

The trees stood in the last sunshine of evening as though they had borrowed their green coats from Paradise; the paths were weeded; the stones had a fresh coat of whitewash; there was not a patch of soil without its plants or seedlings. From every clump of ivy on the old walls of the Castle a thrush seemed to be singing; and every one of them seemed to be singing louder than the rest.

Her sewing idle in her lap, Griselda sat on the door-step, drinking everything in with her clear grey eyes, and at the same time she was thinking too. Not only of Moleskins and of all he had done for her, but of the farmer's son also, who had come part of the way home with her the evening before. And then she began to day-dream.

But it seemed her spirit had been but a moment gone out of her body into this far-away when the tiny sound of stone knocking on stone recalled her to her-self again, and there—in the very last beam of the setting sun—stood the dwarf on the cobbles of the garden path. He told Griselda that his nine days' work for her was done, and that he had come for his wages.

Griselda beckoned him into the kitchen, and there she whispered her thanks again and again for all his help and kindness. She took her last penny out of her purse and put it on the table, then tiptoeing, reached up to the chimney-shelf and lifted down the pewter pot. Even as she did so, her heart turned cold inside her. Not the faintest jingle sounded when she shook it. It seemed light as a feather. With trembling fingers she managed at last to lift the lid and look in. "Oh!" she whispered. "Someone . . ." A dark cloud came over her eyes. The pot was empty.

The dwarf stood in the doorway, his eager cold bright eyes fixed on her face. "Well," he croaked. "Where is my money? Why am I to be kept waiting, young woman? Answer me that!"

Griselda could only stare back at him, the empty pot in her hand. His eyebrows began to jerk up and down

as if with rage, like an orang-outang's. "So it's gone, eh? My pennies are all gone, eh? So you have cheated me! Eh? Eh? *Cheated* me?"

Nothing Griselda could say was of any avail. He refused to listen to her. The more she entreated him only to have patience and she would pay him all she owed him, the more sourly and angrily he stormed at her. And to see the tears rolling down her cheeks on either side of her small nose only worsened his rage.

"I will give you one more day," he bawled at last. "One! I will come back to-morrow at sunset, and every single penny must be ready for me. What I do, I can undo! What I make, I can break! Hai, hai! we shall see!" With that he stumped out into the garden and was gone.

Griselda was so miserable and her mind was in such disorder that she could do nothing for a while but sit, cold and vacant, staring out of the open door. Where could the pennies have gone to? Mice don't eat pennies. Had she been walking in her sleep? Who could have stolen them? And how was she to earn as many more in only one day's work?

And while she sat brooding, there came a *thump*, *thump*, *thump* on the floor over her head. She sprang to her feet, lit a candle by the fire-flames, dabbled her eyes in the bucket of cold water that Old Moleskins had brought in from the well, and took up her grandmother's supper.

"Did you hear any noises in the house to-day, Grannie?" she asked cautiously as she put the bowl of broth into her skinny old hands. At this question the old woman, who was very hungry, fell into a temper. Every single evening, she told Griselda, she had warned her that some strange animal had come rummaging into the house below when she was away working at the farm. "You never kept watch, you never even answered me," she said. "And now it's too late. To-day I have heard nothing."

It was all but dark when, having made the old woman comfortable for the night, Griselda hastened down into the kitchen again. She could not bear to wait until morning. She had made up her mind what to do. Leaving her grandmother drowsy after her broth and nodding off to sleep, she stole out of the house and shut the door gently behind her. Groping her way under the ivied walls into the open she hastened on in the quiet moonlight, climbing as swiftly as she could the steep grassy slope at the cliff's edge. An owl called. From far below she could hear the tide softly gushing on the stones of the beach; and over the sea the sky was alive with stars.

A light was still glimmering at an upper window when she reached the farm. She watched it a while and the shadows moving to and fro across the blind, and at last timidly lifted the knocker and knocked on the door. The farmer himself answered her knock. A candlestick in his hand, he stood there in his shirt sleeves looking out at her over his candle, astonished to find so late a visitor standing there in the starlight, muffled up in a shawl. But he spoke kindly to her. And then and there Griselda poured out her story, though she said not a word about the dwarf.

She told the farmer that she was in great trouble; that, though she couldn't give him any reasons, she must have eight pennies by the next evening. And if only he would lend her them and trust her, she promised him faithfully she would work for just as long as he wanted her to in exchange.

"Well," said the farmer. "That's a queer tale, *that* is! But why not work for four days, and I'll give 'ee the eightpence then." But Griselda shook her head. She told him that this was impossible; that she could not wait, not even for one day.

"See here, then," said the farmer, smiling to himself, though not openly, for he was curious to know what use she was going to make of the money. "I can't give you any work to-morrow, nor be sure of the next day. But supposing there's none for a whole week, if you promise to cut off that gold hair of yours and give me that *then*, you shall have the eight pennies now—this very moment—and no questions asked."

Griselda stood quite still in the doorway, her face pale and grave in the light of the farmer's candle. It seemed that every separate hair she had was stirring upon her head. This all came, she thought, of admiring herself in the duck-pond; and not being more careful with her money; and doing what the dwarf told her to do and not what she thought best. But as it seemed that at any moment the farmer might run in and fetch a pair of shears to cut off her hair there and then, she made her promise; and he himself went back laughing to his wife, and told her what had happened. "She turned as white as a sheet," he said. "And what I'd dearly like to know is what's worriting the poor dear. She's as gentle as the day is long, and her word's as good as her bond. Well, well! But I'll see to it. And we'll have just one lock of that hair, my dear, if only for a keepsake."

"It looks to me", said the farmer's wife, "*that*'ll be for our Simon to say."

When Griselda reached home again—and a sad and solitary walk it had been through the dewy fields above the sea—she went to an old wooden coffer in which she kept her few "treasures". Many of them were remembrances of her mother. And she took out a net for the hair that her mother herself had worn when she was a girl of about the same age as Griselda. Then she sat down in front of a little bare square of looking-glass, braided her hair as close as she could to her head, and drew the net tightly over it. Then she put her purse with the nine pennies in it under her pillow, said her prayers, and got into bed.

For hours she lay listening to the breakers on the shore, solemnly drumming the night away, and watched her own particular star as moment by moment it sparkled on from diamond pane to pane across her lattice window. But when at last she fell asleep, her dreams were scarcely less sorrowful than her waking

She stayed at home the next day in case the dwarf

should come early, but not until sunset did she hear the furtive clatter of his shoes as usual on the stones. She took out her purse to pay him his pennies. He asked her where they had come from. "And why", said he, "have you braided your hair so close and caged it up in a net? Are you frightened the birds will be after it?"

Griselda laughed at this in spite of herself. And she told him that she had promised her hair to a friend, and that she had wound it up tight to her head in order to remind herself that it was not her own any longer, and to keep it safe. At this Old Moleskins himself burst out laughing under the green-berried gooseberry bush—for Griselda had taken him out into the garden lest her grandmother should hear them talking.

"A pretty bargain *that* was!" he said. "But *I* know one even better!" And he promised Griselda that if she would let him snip off but one small lock of her hair he would transport her into the grottoes of the Urchin People under the sea. "And *there*," he said, "if you will work for us for only one hour a day for seven days, you shall have seven times the weight of all your hair in fine solid gold. If, after that, I mean," and he eyed her craftily, "you will promise to come back and stay with us always. And then you shall have a basket of fruit from our secret orchards."

Griselda looked at the dwarf, and then at the small green ripening gooseberries on the bush, and then stared a while in silence at the daisies on the ground. Then she told the dwarf she could not give him a lock of her hair because that was all promised. Instead, she would work for him every day for nine days, free. It was the least she could do, she thought, in return for what he had done for her.

"Well then," said Moleskins, "if it can't be hair it

must be eyelash. Else you will never see the grottoes. An eyelash for your journey-money!"

To this she agreed, and knelt down beside the gooseberry bush, shutting her eyes tight so that he might more easily pluck out one of the lashes that fringed their lids. She felt his stumpy earthy fingers brush across them, and nothing beside.

But when she opened them, and looked out of her body, a change had come upon the scene around her —garden, cottage, castle walls and ruined turrets, cliffs, sea and caves—all had vanished. No evening ray of sun shone here, not the faintest sea-breeze stirred the air. It was a place utterly still, and lay bathed in a half-light pale and green, rilling in from she knew not where. And around her, and above her head, faint colours shimmered in the quarried quartz of the grottoes. And the only sound to be heard was a distant sighing, as of the tide.

There were many trees here, too, in the orchards of the Urchin People, their slim stems rooted in sands as fine and white as hoarfrost. And their branches were laden with fruits of as many colours as there are precious stones. And there was a charm of birds singing, though Griselda could see none. The very air seemed thin and fine in this dim and sea-green light: the only other sound to be heard was a faint babbling of water among the rocks, water which lost itself in the sands of the orchard.

The dwarf had brought out some little rush baskets, and told Griselda what she must do. "Gather up the fallen fruit," he said, "but pick none from the branches, and sort it out each according to its kind and colour, one colour into each of the baskets. But be sure not to climb into the trees nor shake them. And when your hour is finished I will come again."

Griselda at once set to work. Though the branches overhead were thick with fruit, there were as yet not many that had fallen, and it seemed at first it would take her but a few moments to sort them out into their baskets. But the thin air and twilight of the grotto made her drowsy, and as she stooped again and yet again to pick up the fruit, her eyelids drooped so heavily that at any moment she feared she would fall asleep. And if once she fell asleep what might not happen then? Would she ever win back to earth again? Was this all nothing but a dream? She refreshed her eyes in the trickle of snow-cold water rilling down from the rocks; and now she fancied she heard a faint metallic noise as of knocking and hammering and small voices in the distance. But even when all the fallen fruits had been sorted out into her baskets, emerald-green, orange, amethyst, crystal and blue, her work was not done. For the moment she sat down to rest, yet another of the fruits would plump down softly as an apple into deep grass upon the sand beneath it, and she had to hasten away to put it into its basket.

When the dwarf came back he looked about him to see that no fruits had been left lying in the sand. He squinnied here, he squinnied there, and even turned over the fruits in the baskets to see that they had been sorted right. "Well, Griselda," he said at last, and it was the first time he had used her name, "what's well done is done for good. And here's the penny for your wages."

There was a stealthy gleam in his eyes as he softly fumbled with his fingers in the old moleskin pouch that hung at his side, and fetched out his penny. Griselda held out her hand, and he put the penny into its palm, still watching her. She looked at it—and looked again.

It was an old, thick, battered penny, and the king's image on it had been worn very faint. It had a slightly crooked edge, too, and there was a hole in it. There could be no doubt of it—this was the penny the farmer had given her, "for luck". Until now Griselda had not realized that she had for a moment suspected it might be Old Moleskins himself who had stolen his pennies out of the pewter pot. Now she was sure of it. She continued to stare at the penny, yet said nothing. After all, she was thinking to herself, the money in the pot belonged to him. He had a right to it. You cannot steal what is yours already! But then, a lie is almost as bad as stealing. Perhaps he hadn't meant it to be a lie. Perhaps he merely wanted to see what she might say and do. That would still be a lie but not such a wicked lie. Perhaps since he wasn't *quite* human he couldn't in any case tell *quite* a lie. Perhaps it was only a dwarf lie, though his kindness to her had certainly not been only dwarf kindness! She smiled to herself at this; lifted up her face again, and seeing the dwarf still watching her, smiled at him also. And she thanked him.

At this he burst out laughing, till the roof and walls of the grotto echoed with the cackle of it, and at least half a dozen of the grotto fruits dropped from their twigs and thumped softly down into the sand. "Aha," he cried, "what did I tell you? Weep no more, Griselda. That is one penny, and here are the others." He took them out of his pouch, and counted them into her hand, and the eight pennies too that she had given him but a little while before; and as he did so, he sang out in a high quavering voice like a child's:

"*Never whatever the humans say*
Have the Urchin Folk worked for any man's pay.

Ah, Griselda," he said, "if we could keep you, you would scarcely ever have to work at all. No churning and weeding, no sewing and scrubbing, no cooking or polishing, sighing or sobbing; you should be for ever happy and for ever young. And you wouldn't have to scissor off a single snippet of your yellow hair!"

Griselda looked at him in the still green light and faintly shook her head. But she made a bargain with him none the less that every year she would work in the grottoes for the Urchin People—if he would come to fetch her—for one whole summer's day. So this was the bargain between them.

And he took out of his breeches' pocket a thick gold piece, about the size of an English crown piece, and put it into her hand. On the one side of it the image of a mermaid was stamped, on the other a little fruit tree growing out of a mound of sand and knobbed with tiny fruits. "That's for a keepsake," he said. And he himself took one of each kind of the orchard fruits out of their baskets and put them into another. "And since 'no pay' is *no* pay," he went on, "stoop, Griselda, and I'll give you your eyelash back again."

Griselda knelt down in the sand, and once more the earthy fingers brushed over her eyelids. The next instant all was dark; and a thin chill wind was stirring on her cheek. She opened her eyes to find herself alone again under the night-sky, and—as though she had been overtaken by the strangeness of a dream—kneeling on the dew-damped mould of her familiar garden under the stars. But for proof that what had happened was no dream, the gold piece stamped with the images of the mermaid and the leafy tree was still clasped in her hand, and in the other was the basket of fruits.

As for the eyelash, since Griselda had never counted

how many she had before Old Moleskins plucked one out, she could never tell for certain if it had been put back. But when she told Simon, the farmer's son, that there *might* be one missing—and she could tell him no more because of her promise to the dwarf—he counted them over again and again. And though he failed to make the total come to the same number twice, he assured Griselda that there couldn't possibly ever have been room for another. And Griselda gave him the green one of the grotto fruits she had brought him for a present from out of the dwarf's basket. This too was for a keepsake. "It's as hard as a stone," he said. "Do we eat it, Griselda?" But hard though it was, there must have been a curious magic in it, for as they sat there together under the willow tree by the duck-pond, it was as if they had been transported not into the grottoes of the Urchin People under the sea, but clean back into the Garden of Eden.

As for Griselda's hair, there it shone as thick as ever on her head. And as for the farmer, he refused every single penny of the eightpence.

"It's a queer thing to me, mother," he was saying to his wife at this very moment, as they sat together on either side of the kitchen fire—just as they were accustomed to sit even in the height of summertime—"it's a queer thing to me that this very farm of ours once belonged to that young woman's great-great-grandfather!" He took a long whiff of his pipe. "And what *I* says is that them who once had, when they gets again, should know how to *keep*."

"Ay, George," said she, and she said no more.

The Three Sleeping Boys of Warwickshire

In a long, low-ceiled, white-washed room on the upper floor of a red-brick building in Pleasant Street, Cheriton, ranged there in their glazed cases, is a collection of shells, conchs, seaweeds, sea-flowers, corals, fossils, goggling fish, stuffed birds—sea and land—and 'mermaids'. Coffers, too, and anchors, and old guns, and lumps of amber and ore and quartz. All sorts of outlandish oddities, too, curiosities and junk. And there for years and years—the narrow windows, with their carved brick fruits and flowers and old leaden gutters, showering the day's light upon their still retreat—there for years and years slumbered on in their great glass case the Three Sleeping Boys of Warwickshire. The tale of them goes a long way back. But so, too, do most tales, sad or merry, if only you will follow them up.

About the year 1600, when Queen Elizabeth was sixty-seven, and William Shakespeare was writing his play called "Julius Caesar", there died, twenty-four miles from Stratford-on-Avon, a rich miller—John James Nollykins by name. His was the handsomest mill in Warwickshire. But none of his neighbours—or none at least of his poorer neighbours—could abide the sight of him. He was a morose, close-fisted, pitiless old man. He cheated his customers and had no mercy for those whom he enticed into his clutches.

As he grew older he had grown ever more mean and churlish until at last he had even begun to starve his own horses. Though he died rich, then, few of his neighbours mourned him much. And as soon as he was gone his money began to go too. His three sons gobbled up what he had left behind him, as jackals gobble up a lion's left supper-bones. It slipped through their fingers like sand through a sieve. They drank, they diced, they gambled high and low. They danced, and capered and feasted in their finery; but they hardly knew offal from grain. Pretty soon they began to lose not only their father's trade but also all his savings. Their customers said that there was not only dust but stones in the flour; and tares too. It was fusty; it smelt mousey. What cared they? They took their terriers rat-hunting, but that was for the sake of the sport and not of the flour. Everything about the Mill got shabbier and shabbier—went to rack and ruin. The sails were patched. They clacked in the wind. The rain drove in. There were blossoming weeds in the millstream and dam where should have been nothing but crystal water. And when their poorer customers complained, they were greeted with drunken jeers and mockery.

At length, three or four years after the death of the miller's last poor half-starved mare, his sons were ruined. They would have been ruined just the same if, as one foul windy night they sat drinking and singing together in the Mill-house, the youngest of them had not knocked over the smoking lamp on the table, and so burned the Mill to the ground.

The eldest—with what he could pick up—went off to Sea, and to foreign parts, and died of yellow fever in Tobago. The second son was taken in by an uncle who was a goldsmith in London. But he was so stupid and indolent that he broke more than he mended; and at last, by swallowing an exquisitely carved peach-stone from China, which had been brought back to Italy by Marco Polo, so enraged his master that he turned him off then and there. He went East and became a fishmonger in Ratcliff Highway, with a shop like a booth, and a long board in front of it. But he neglected this trade too, and at last became a man-of-all-work (or of none) at the old Globe Theatre in Southwark, where he saw Shakespeare dressed up as the ghost in "Hamlet" and was all but killed as if by accident while taking the part of the Second Murderer in "Macbeth".

The youngest son, named Jeremy, married the rich widow of a saddler. She was the owner of a fine gabled house in the High Street of the flourishing town of Cheriton—some eight miles from Bishops Hitchingworth. He had all the few good looks of the family, but he was sly and crafty and hard. The first thing he did after he came home from his honeymoon was to paint in a long red nose to the portrait of the saddler. The next thing he did was to drown his wife's cat in the water-butt, because he said the starveling had stolen the cheese. The third thing he did was to burn her best Sunday bonnet, then her wig—to keep it company. How she could bear to go on living with him is a mystery. Nevertheless she did.

This Jeremy had three sons: Job, John and (another) Jeremy. But he did not flourish. Far from it. The family went "down the ladder", rung by rung, until at long last it reached the bottom. Then it began to climb up again. But Jeremy's children did best. His youngest daughter married a well-to-do knacker, and *their* only son (yet another Jeremy), though he ran away from home because he hated water-gruel and suet pudding, went into business as assistant to the chief sweep in Cheriton. And, at last, having by his craft and cunning and early rising and hard-working inherited his master's business, he bought his great-uncle's fine gabled house, and became Master Chimney-Sweep and "Sweep by Appointment", to the Mayor and Corporation and the Lords of three neighbouring Manors. And *he* never married at all. In spite of his hard childhood, in spite of the kindness shown him by his master, in spite of his good fortune with the three Lords of the Manor, he was a skinflint and a pick-halfpenny. He had an enormous brush over his door, a fine brass knocker, and—though considering all things, he had mighty few friends—he was the best, as well as the richest master-sweep in those parts.

But a good deal of his money and in later years most of his praise was due to his three small orphan 'prentices—Tom, Dick and Harry. In those days, hearths and fireplaces were as large as little rooms or chambers, or at any rate, as large as large cupboards or closets. They had wide warm comfortable ingle-nooks, and the chimneys were like deep wells running up to the roof, sometimes narrowing or angling off towards the top. And these chimneys were swept by hand.

Jeremy's 'prentices, then, had to climb up and up, from sooty brick to brick with a brush, and sweep till they were as black as blackest blackamoors, inside and out. Soot, soot, soot! Eyes, mouth, ears and nose. And now and then the bricks were scorching hot, and their hands got blistered. And now and then they were all but suffocated in the narrow juts. And once in a while were nearly wedged there, to dry like mummies in the dark. And sometimes, in the midst of the smother, a leg would slip, and down they would come tumbling like apples out of a tree or hailstones out of a cloud in April.

And Jeremy Nollykins, after tying up all the money they brought him in fat canvas and leather bags, served them out water-gruel for supper, and water-gruel for breakfast. For dinner on Tuesdays and Thursdays he gave them slabs of suet-pudding with lumps of suet in it like pale amber beads; what he called soup on Mondays and Wednesdays and Fridays; and a bit of catsmeat (bought cheap from his second cousin) on Sundays. But then you can't climb chimneys on *no* meat. On Saturdays they had piping-hot pease-pudding and pottage: because on Saturdays the Mayor's man might look in. You would hardly believe it: but in spite of such poor mean living, in spite of their burns and their bruises, and the soot in their eyes and lungs and in their close lint-coloured hair, these three small boys, Tom, Dick and Harry, managed to keep their spirits up. They even rubbed their cheeks rosy after the week's soot had been washed off under the pump on a Saturday night.

They were like Tom Dacre in the poem:

. . . There's little Tom Dacre, who cried when his head
That curled like a lamb's back was shav'd: so I said
"Hush, Tom! never mind it for when your head's bare
You know that the soot cannot spoil your white hair."

And so he was quiet, and that very night
As Tom was a-sleeping, he had such a sight!
That thousands of sleepers, Dick, Joe, Ned, and Jack
Were all of them lock'd up in coffins of black. . . .

Still, they always said "Mum" to the great ladies and "Mistress" to the maids, and they kept their manners even when some crabbed old woman said they were owdacious, or imperent, or mischeevious. And sometimes a goodwife would give them a slice of bread pudding, or a mug of milk, or a baked potato, or perhaps a pocket-full of cookies or a slice of white bread (which did not remain white for very long). And now and then, even a sip of elderberry wine. After all, even half-starved sparrows sometimes find tit-bits, and it's not the hungry who enjoy their victuals least.

When they *could* scuttle away too, they would bolt off between their jobs to go paddling in the river, or bird-nesting in the woods, or climbing in an old stone quarry not very far from the town. It was lovely wooded country thereabouts—near ancient Cheriton.

Whether they played truant or not, Jeremy Nollykins the Fourth—Old Noll, as his neighbours called him—used to beat them morning, noon and night. He believed in the rod. He said it was the finest sauce for the saucy. Tom, Dick and Harry pretty well hated old Noll: and that's a bad thing enough. But, on the other hand, they were far too much alive and hearty and happy when they were not being beaten, and they were much too hungry even over their water-gruel to *think* or to brood over how much they hated him: which would have been a very much worse.

In sober fact—with their bright glittering eyes and round cheeks and sharp white teeth, and in spite of their skinny ribs and blistered hands, they were a merry trio. As soon as ever their teeth stopped chattering with the cold, and their bodies stopped smarting from Old Noll's sauce, and their eyes from the soot; they were laughing and talking and whistling and champing, like grasshoppers in June or starlings in September. And though they sometimes quarrelled and fought together, bit and scratched too, never having been taught to fight fair, they were very good friends. Now and again too they shinned up a farmer's fruit-trees to have a taste of his green apples. Now and again they played tricks on old women. But what lively little chimney-sweeps wouldn't?

They were three young ragamuffins, as wild as colts, as nimble as kids, though a good deal blacker. And, however hard he tried, Old Noll never managed to break them in. Never. And at night they slept as calm and deep as cradled babies—all three of them laid in a row up in an attic under the roof on an immense wide palliasse or mattress of straw, with a straw bolster and a couple of pieces of old sacking for blankets each.

Now Old Noll, simply perhaps because he was—both by nature as well as by long practice—a mean old

curmudgeonly miser, hated to see anybody merry, or happy, or even fat. There were moments when he would have liked to skin his three 'prentices alive. But then he wanted to get out of them all the work he could. So he was compelled to give them *that* much to eat. He had to keep them alive—or the Mayor's man would ask Why. Still, it enraged him that he could not keep their natural spirits down; that however much he beat them they "came up smiling". It enraged him to know in his heart (or whatever took its place) that though—when they had nothing better to do, or were smarting from his rod and pickle—they detested him, they yet had never done him an ill-turn.

Every day he would gloat on them as they came clattering down to their water-gruel just as Giant Despair gloated on Faithful and Christian in the dungeon. And sometimes at night he would creep up to their bare draughty attic, and the stars or the moon would show him the three of them lying there fast asleep on their straw mattress, the sacking kicked off, and on their faces a faint far-away smile as if their dreams were as peaceful as the swans in the Islands of the Blest. It enraged him. What could the little urchins be dreaming about? What made ugly little blackamoors grin even in their sleep? You can thwack a wake boy, but you can't thwack a dreamer; not at least while he *is* dreaming. So here Old Noll was helpless. He could only grind his teeth at the sight of them. Poor Old Noll.

He ground his teeth more than ever when he first heard the music in the night. And he might never have heard it at all if hunger hadn't made him a mighty bad sleeper himself. A few restless hours was the most he got, even in winter. And if Tom, Dick and Harry had ever peeped in on *him* as he lay in his four-post bed, they would have seen no smile on his old sunken face, with its long nose and long chin and straggling hair—but only a sort of horrifying darkness. They might even have pitied him, stretched out there, with nightmare twisting and contorting his sharp features, and his bony fingers continually on the twitch.

Because, then, Old Noll could not sleep of nights, he would sometimes let himself out of his silent house to walk the streets. And while so walking, he would look up at his neighbours' windows, glossily dark beneath the night-sky, and he would curse them for being more comfortable than he. It was as if instead of marrow he had malice in his bones, and there is no fattening on that.

Now one night, for the first time in his life, except when he broke his leg at eighteen, Old Noll had been unable to sleep at all. It was a clear mild night with no wind, and a fine mild scrap of a moon was in the west, and the stars shone bright. There was always a sweet balmy air in Cheriton, borne in from the meadows that then stretched in within a few furlongs of the town; and so silent was the hour you could almost hear the rippling of the river among its osiers that far away.

And as Old Nollykins was sitting like a gaunt shadow all by himself on the first milestone that comes into the town—and he was too niggardly even to smoke a pipe of tobacco—a faint easy wind came drifting along the street. And then on the wind a fainter music—a music which at first scarcely seemed to be a music at all. None the less it continued on and on, and at last so rilled and trembled in the air that even Old Nollykins, who was now pretty hard of hearing, caught the strains and recognized the melody. It came steadily nearer,

that music—a twangling and a tootling and a horning, a breathing as of shawms, waxing merrier and merrier in the quick mild night October air:

Girls and boys come out to play.
The moon doth shine as bright as day;
Leave your supper, and leave your sleep,
And come with your playfellows into the street. . . .

Girls and boys come out to play: on and on and on, now faint now shrill, now in a sudden rallying burst of sound as if it came from out of the skies. Not that the moon just then was shining as bright as day. It was but barely in its first quarter. It resembled a bent bit of intensely shining copper down low among the stars: or a gold basin, of which little more than the edge showed, resting a-tilt. But little moon or none, the shapes that were now hastening along the street, running and hopping and skipping and skirring and dancing, had heard the summons, had obeyed the call. From by-lane and alley, court, porch and house-door the children of Cheriton had come pouring out like water-streams in spring-time. Running, skipping, hopping, dancing, they kept time to the tune. Old Noll fairly gasped with astonishment as he watched them. What a dreadful tale to tell—and all the comfortable and respectable folks of Cheriton fast asleep in their beds! To think such innocents could be such wicked deceivers! To think that gluttonous and grubby errand and shop and boot-and-shoe and pot boys could look so clean and nimble and happy and free. He shivered; partly because of his age and the night air, and part with rage.

But real enough though these young skip-by-nights appeared to be, there were three queer things about them. First, there was not the faintest sound of doors opening or shutting, or casement windows being thrust open with a squeal of the iron rod. Next, there was not the faintest rumour of footsteps even, though at least half the children of Cheriton were now bounding along the street, like autumn leaves in the wind, and all with their faces towards the East and the water-meadows. And last, though Noll could see the very eyes in their faces in the faint luminousness of starshine and little moon, not a single one of that mad young company turned head to look at him, or showed the least sign of knowing that he was there. Clockwork images

of wood or wax could not have ignored him more completely.

Old Noll, after feeling at first startled, flabbergasted, a little frightened even, was now in a fury. His few old teeth began to grind together as lustily as had the mill-stones of Jeremy the First when he was rich and prosperous. Nor was his rage diminished when, lo and behold, even as he turned his head, out of his own narrow porch with its three rounded steps and fluted shell of wood above it, came leaping along who but his own three half-starved 'prentices, Tom, Dick and Harry—now seemingly nine-year-olds as plump and comely to see as if they had been fed on the fat of the land, as if they had never never in the whole of their lives so much as tasted rod-sauce. Their mouths were opening and shutting, too, as if they were whooping calls one to the other and to their other street-mates, though no sound came from them. They snapped their fingers in the air. They came cavorting and skirling along in their naked feet to the strains of the music as if bruised elbows, scorched shins, cramped muscles and iron-bound clogs had never once pestered their young souls. Yet not a sound, not a whisper, not a footfall could the deaf old man hear—nothing but that sweet, shrill and infuriating music.

In a few minutes the streets were empty, a thin fleece of cloud had drawn across the moon, and only one small straggler was still in sight, a grandson of the Mayor. He was last merely because he was least, and had nobody to take care of him. And Old Noll, having watched this last night-truant out of sight, staring at him with eyes like marbles beneath his bony brows, hobbled back across the street to his own house, and after pausing awhile at the nearest doorpost to gnaw his beard and think what next was to be done, climbed his three flights of shallow oak stairs until he came to the uppermost landing under the roof. There at last with infinite caution he lifted the pin of the door of the attic and peered in on what he supposed would be an empty bed. Empty! Not a bit of it! Lying there asleep, in the dim starlight of the dusty dormer window, he could see as plain as can be the motionless shapes of his three 'prentices, breathing on so calmly in midnight's deepmost slumber that he even ventured to fetch in a tallow candle in a pewter stick in order that he might examine them more closely.

In its smoky beams he searched the three young slumbering faces. They showed no sign that the old skinflint was stooping as close over them as a bird-snarer over his nets. There were smears of soot even on their eye-lids and the fine dust of it lay thick on the flaxen lamb's-wool of their close-shorn heads. They were smiling away, gently and distantly as if they were sitting in their dreams in some wonderful orchard, supping up strawberries and cream; as though the spirits within them were untellably happy though their bodies were as fast asleep as humming-tops or honey-bees in winter.

Stair by stair Old Nollykins crept down again, blew out his candle, and sat down on his bed to think. He was a cunning old miser, which is as far away from being generous and wise as the full moon is from a farthing dip. His fingers had itched to wake his three sleeping chimney-boys with a smart taste of his rod, just to "larn them a lesson". He hated to think of the quiet happy smile resting upon their faces while the shadow-shapes or ghosts of them were out and away, pranking and gallivanting in the green water-meadows beyond the town. How was he to know that his dimming eyes had not deluded him? Supposing he went off to the Mayor himself in the morning and told his midnight tale, who would believe it? High and low, everybody hated him, and as like as not they would shut him up in the town jail for a madman, or burn his house about his ears supposing him to be a wizard. "No, no, no!" he muttered to himself. "We must watch and wait, friend Jeremy, and see what we *shall* see."

Next morning his three 'prentices, Tom, Dick and Harry, were up and about as sprightly as ever, a full hour before daybreak. You might have supposed from their shining eyes and apple cheeks that they had just come back from a long holiday on the blissful plains of paradise. Away they tumbled—merry as frogs—to work, with their brushes and bags, still munching away at their gritty oatcakes—three parts bran to one of meal.

So intent had Old Noll been on watching from his chimney-corner what he could see in their faces at breakfast, and on trying to overhear what they were whispering to each other, that he forgot to give them their usual morning dose of stick. But not a word had been uttered about the music or the dancing or the company at the water-meadows. They just talked their usual scatter-brained gibberish to one another—except when they saw that the old creature was watching them; and he was speedily convinced that whatever adventures their dream-shapes may have had in the night-hours, this had left no impression on their waking minds.

Poor Old Noll. An echo of that music and the sight he had seen kept him awake for many a night after, and his body was already shrunken up by age and his miserly habits to nothing much more substantial than a bag of animated bones. And yet all his watching was in vain. So weary and hungry for sleep did he become, that when at last the hunter's moon shone at its brightest and roundest over the roofs of Cheriton, he nodded off in his chair. He was roused a few hours afterwards by a faint glow in his room that was certainly not moonlight, for it came from out of the black dingy staircase passage. Instantly he was wide awake—but too late. For, even as he peeped through the door-crack, there flitted past his three small 'prentices—just the ghosts or the spirits or the dream-shapes of them—faring merrily away. They passed him softer than a breeze through a willow tree and were out of sight down the staircase before he could stir.

The morning after the morning after that, when Tom, Dick and Harry woke up at dawn on their mattress, there was a wonderful rare smell in the air. They sniffed it greedily as they looked at one another in the creeping light of daybreak. And sure enough, as soon as they were in their ragged jackets and had got down to their breakfast, the old woman who came to the house every morning to do an hour or two's charing for Old Nollykins, came waddling up to the kitchen table with a frying-pan of bacon frizzling in its fat.

"There, me boys," said Old Noll, rubbing his hands together with a cringing smile, "there's a rasher of bacon for ye all, and sop in the pan to keep the cold out, after that long night-run in the moonlight."

He creaked up his eyes at them, finger on nose; but all three of them, perched up there on their wooden stools the other side of the table, only paused an instant in the first polishing up of their plates with a crust of bread to stare at him with such an innocent astonishment on their young faces that he was perfectly sure they had no notion of what he meant.

"Aha," says he, "do ye never dream, me boys, tucked up snug under the roof in that comfortable bed of yours? D'ye never dream?—never hear a bit of a tune calling, or maybe see what's called a nightmare? Lordee, when I was young there never went a night but had summat of a dream to it."

"Dream!" said they, and looked at one another with their mouths half open. "Why, if you ax me, Master," says Tom, "I dreamed last night it was all bright moonshine, and me sitting at supper with the gentry."

"And I," says Dick, "I dreamed I was dancing under trees and bushes all covered over with flowers. And I could hear 'em playing on harps and whistles."

"And me," says Harry, "I dreamed I was by a river, and a leddy came out by a green place near the water and took hold of my hand. I suppose, Master, it must have been my mammie, though I never seed her as I knows on."

At all this the cringing smile on Old Nollykins' face set like grease in a dish, because of the rage in his mind underneath. And he leaped up from where he sat beside the skinny little fire in the immense kitchen hearth. " 'Gentry'! 'Harps'! 'Mammie'!" he shouted, "you brazen, ungrateful, greedy little deevils. Be off with ye, or ye shall have such a taste of the stick as will put ye to sleep for good and all."

And almost before they had time to snatch up their bags and their besoms, he had chased them out of the house. So there in the little alley beside the garden, sheltering as close to its wall as they could from the cold rain that was falling, they must needs stand chattering together like drenched jackdaws, waiting for the angry old man to come out and to send them about the business of the day.

But Old Nollykins' dish of bacon fat had not been altogether wasted. He knew now that the young rapscallions only *dreamed* their nocturnal adventures, and were not in the least aware that they themselves in actual shadow-shape went off by night to the trysting-place of all Cheriton's children to dance and feast and find delight. But he continued to keep watch, and would again and again spy in on his three 'prentices laid together asleep on their mattress on the attic floor, in the hope of catching them in the act of stealing out. But though at times he discerned that same quiet smile upon their faces, shining none the less serenely for the white gutter-marks of tears on their sooty cheeks, for weeks together he failed to catch any repetition of the strains of the strange music or the faintest whisper of their dream-shapes coming and going on the wooden stairs.

Nevertheless, the more he brooded on what he had seen, the more he hated the three urchins, and the more bitterly he resented their merry ways. The one thing he could not decide in his mind was whether when next, if ever, he caught them at their midnight tricks, he should at once set about their slumbering bodies with his stick or should wait until their dream-wraiths were safely away and then try to prevent them from coming back. Then indeed they might be at his mercy.

Now there was an old crone in Cheriton who was reputed to be a witch. She lived in a stone hovel at the far end of a crooked alley that ran beside the very walls of Old Nollykins' fine gabled house. And Old Nollykins, almost worn to a shadow, knocked one dark evening at her door. She might have been the old man's grandmother as she sat there, hunched up in her corner beside the great iron pot simmering over the fire. He mumbled out his story about his three "thieving, godless little brats", and then sat haggling over the price he should pay for her counsel. And even then he hoped to cheat her. At last he put his crown in her shrunken paw.

Waken a sleeper, she told him, before his dream-shape can get back into his mortal frame, it's as like as not to be sudden death. But keep the wandering dream-shape out *without* rousing his sleeping body, then he may for ever more be your slave, and will never grow any older. And what may keep a human's dream-shape out—or animal's either—she said, is a love-knot of iron the wrong way up or a rusty horseshoe upside down, or a twisted wreath of elder and ash fastened up with an iron nail over the keyhole—and every window shut. Brick walls and stone and wood are nothing to such wanderers. But they can't abide iron. And what she said was partly true and partly false; and it was in part false because the foolish old man had refused to pay the crone her full price.

Now Old Nollykins knew well that there was only a wooden latch to his door, because he had been too much of a skinflint to pay for one of the new iron locks to be fixed on. He had no fear of thieves, because he had so hidden his money that no thief on earth would be able to find it, not if he searched for a week. So he asked the old woman again, to make doubly sure, how long a natural human creature would live and work if his dream-shape never got back. "Why, that," she cheepered, leering up at him out of her wizened old face, "that depends how young they be; what's the blood, and what's the heart. Take 'em in the first bloom," she said, "and so they keeps". She had long ago seen what the old man was after, and had no more love for him than for his three noisy whooping chimney-sweeps.

So Old Nollykins very unwillingly put another bit of money into her skinny palm and went back to his house, not knowing that the old woman, to avenge herself on his skinflint ways, had told him only half the story. That evening the three 'prentices had a rare game of hide-and-seek together in the many-roomed old rat-holed house; for their master had gone out. The moment they heard his shuffling footsteps in the porch they scampered off to bed, and were to all appearance fast asleep before he could look in on them.

And Old Nollykins had brought back with him some switches of elder and ash, a tenpenny nail and an old key, and a cracked horseshoe. And, strange to say, the iron key which he had bought from a dealer in broken metal had once been the key of the Mill of rich old Jeremy the First at Stratford-on-Avon. He pondered half that night on what the old woman had said, and "surely", said he to himself, "their blood's fresh enough, my old stick keeps them out of mischief, and what is better for a green young body than a long day's work and not too much to eat, and an airy lodging for the night?" The cunning old creature supposed indeed, that if only by this sorcery and hugger-mugger he could keep their wandering dream-shapes from their bodies for good and all, his three young 'prentices would never age, never weary, but stay lusty and nimble perhaps for a century. Ay, he would use them as long as he wanted them, and sell them before he died. *He'd* teach them to play truant at night, when honest folk were snoring in their beds. For the first time for weeks his mingy supper off a crust and a ham-bone and a mug of water had tasted like manna come down from the skies.

The very next day chanced to be St. Nicholas's Day. And those were the times of old English winters. Already a fine scattering of snow was on the ground, like tiny white lumps of sago, and the rivers and ponds were frozen hard as iron. Better still, there was all but a fine full moon that night, and the puddles in Cheriton High Street shone like Chinese crystal in the beams slanting down on them from between the eaves of the houses.

For five long hours of dark, after his seven o'clock supper, Old Nollykins managed to keep himself awake. Then, a little before midnight, having assured himself that his three 'prentices were sound asleep in their bed, he groped downstairs again, gently lifted the latch and looked out. There was never such a shining scene before. The snow on the roofs and gables and carved stone-work of the houses gleamed white and smooth as the finest millers' meal. There was not a soul, not even a cat, to be seen in the long stretch of the lampless street. And the stars in the grey-blue sky gleamed like dewdrops on a thorn.

Sure enough, as soon as ever the last stroke of midnight had sounded from St. Andrew's tower, there came faintly wreathing its way out of the distance the same shrill penetrating strains of the ancient tune. Lord bless me, if Old Nollykins had had but one sole drop of the blood of his own youth left in his veins he could not have resisted dancing his old bones out of his body down his steps and into the crudded High Street at the sound of it:

Girls and boys come out to play,
The moon doth shine as bright as day;
Leave your supper, and leave your sleep,
And come with your playfellows into the street.

But, instead, he shuffled like a rat hastily back into the house again; pushed himself in close under the staircase; and waited—leaving the door ajar.

Ho, ho, what's that? Faint flitting lights were now showing in the street, and a sound as of little unhuman cries, and in a minute or two the music loudened so that an old glass case on a table nearby containing the model of a brig which had belonged to Old Nollykins's wicked grandfather who had died in Tobago, fairly rang to the marvellous stirrings on the air. And down helter-skelter from their bed, just as they had slipped in under its sacking—in their breeches and rags of day-shirts, barefoot, came whiffling from stair to stair the ghosts of his three small 'prentices. Old Nollykins hardly had time enough to see the wonderful smile on them, to catch the gleam of the grinning white teeth shining beneath their parted lips, before they were out and away.

Shivering all over, as if with a palsy, the old man hastened up the staircase, and in a minute or two the vacant house resounded with the strokes of his hammer as he drove in the tenpenny nail into the keyhole above the attic door, and hung up key and horseshoe by their strings. This done, he lowered his hammer and listened. Not the faintest whisper, sigh or squeak came from within. But in dread of what he might see he dared not open the door.

Instead, curiosity overcame him. Wrapping a cloak round his skinny shoulders he hurried out into the street. Sure enough, here, there, everywhere in the snow and hoarfrost were footprints—traces at any rate distinct enough for *his* envious eyes, though they were hardly more than those of the skirring of a hungry bird's wing on the surface of the snow. And fondly supposing in his simplicity that he had now safely cheated his 'prentices, that for ever more their poor young empty bodies would be at his beck and call, Old Noll determined to follow away out of the town and into the water-meadows the dream-shapes of the children now all of them out of sight. On and on he went till his breath was whistling in his lungs and he could scarcely drag one foot after the other.

And he came at last to where, in a loop of the Itchen, its waters shining like glass in the moon, there was a circle of pollard and stunted willows. And there, in the lush and frosty grasses was a wonderful company assembled, and unearthly music ascending, it seemed, from out of the bowels of a mound nearby, called Caesar's Camp. And he heard a multitude of voices and singing from within. And all about the meadow wandered in joy the sleep-shapes not only of the children from Cheriton, but from the farms and cottages and gipsy camps for miles around. Sheep were there too, their yellow eyes gleaming in the moon as he trod past them. But none paid any heed to the children or to the "strangers" who had called them out of their dreams.

Strange indeed were these strangers: of middle height, with garments like spider-web, their straight hair of the colour of straw falling gently on either side their narrow cheeks, so that it looked at first glimpse as if they were grey-beards. And as they trod on their narrow feet, the frozen grasses scarcely stirring beneath them, they turned their faces from side to side, looking at the children. And then a fairness that knows no change showed in their features, and their eyes were of a faint flame like that of sea-water on nights of thunder when the tide gently lays its incoming ripples on some wide flat sandy strand of the sea.

And at sight of them Old Nollykins began to be mortally afraid. Not a sign was there of Tom, Dick or Harry. They must have gone into the sonorous mound —maybe were feasting there, if dream-shapes feast. The twangling and trumpeting and incessant music made his head spin round. He peered about for a hiding-place, and at length made his way to one of the old gnarled willows beside the icy stream. There he might have remained safe and sound till morning, if the frost, as he dragged himself up a little way into the lower branches of the tree, had not risen into his nostrils and made him sneeze. There indeed he might have remained safe and sound if he had *merely* sneezed, for an old man's sneeze is not much unlike an old sheep's wheezy winter cough. But such was the poor old man's alarm and terror at the company he had stumbled into that he cried, "God bless us!" after his sneeze—just as his mother had taught him to do.

That was the end of wicked old Nollykins; this was his first step on the long road of repentance. For the next thing he remembered was opening his eyes in the first glimpse of stealing dawn and finding himself perched up in the boughs of a leafless willow-tree, a thin mist swathing the low-lying water-meadows, the sheep gently browsing in the grasses, leaving green marks in the frosty grass as they munched onwards. And such an ache and ague was in Old Noll's bones as he had never, since he was swaddled, felt before. It was as if every frosty switch of every un-polled willow in that gaunt fairy circle by the Itchen had been belabouring him of its own free will the whole night long. His heart and courage were gone. Sighing and groaning, he lowered himself into the meadow, and by the help of a fallen branch for staff made his way at last back into the town.

It was early yet even for the milkmaids, though cocks were crowing from their frosty perches, and the red of the coming sun inflamed the eastern skies. He groped into his house and shut the door. With many rests on the way from stair to stair he hoisted himself up, though every movement seemed to wrench him joint from joint, until at last he reached the attic door. He pressed his long ear against the panel and listened a moment. Not a sound. Then stealthily pushing it open inch by inch, he thrust forward his shuddering head and looked in.

The ruddy light in the East was steadily increasing, and had even pierced through the grimy panes of the dormer window as though to light up the faces of his small chimney-sweeps. It was a Sunday morning and the three faces and lamb's-wool heads showed no trace of the week's soot. But while at other times on spying in at them it looked to Old Nollykins as if their smiling faces were made of wax, now they might be of alabaster. For each one of the three—Tom, Dick and Harry—was lying on his back, their chapped, soot-roughened hands with the torn and broken nails resting on either side of their bodies. No smile now touched their features, but only a solemn quietude as of images eternally at rest. And such was the aspect of the three children that even Old Nollykins dared not attempt to waken them because he knew in his heart that no earthly rod would ever now bestir them out of this sound slumber. Not at least until their spirits had won home again. And the soured old crone was not likely to aid him in that.

He cursed the old woman, battering on her crazy door, but she paid him no heed. And at last, when the Cheriton Church bells began ringing the people to morning service, there was nothing for it, if there was any hope of saving his neck, but to go off to the Mayor's man, dragging himself along the street on a couple of sticks, to tell him that his 'prentices were dead.

Dead they were not, however. The Mayor's man fetched a doctor, and the doctor, after putting a sort of wooden trumpet to their chests, asseverated that there was a stirring under the cage of their ribs. They were fallen into a trance, he said. What is called a *catalepsy*. It was a dreamlike seizure that would presently pass away. But though the old midwife the doctor called in heated up salt, for salt-bags, and hour by hour put a hot brick fresh from the fire to each 'prentice's stone-cold feet, by not a flutter of an eyelid nor the faintest of sighs did any one of the three prove that he was alive or could heed.

There they lay, on their straw pallet, motionless as mummies, still and serene, lovely as any mother might wish, with their solemn Sunday-morning soap-polished cheeks and noses and foreheads and chins, and as irresponsive as cherubs made of stone.

And the Mayor of the Town, after listening to all Old Nollykins could say, fined him Five Bags of Guineas for allowing his three 'prentices to fall into a catalepsy for want of decent food and nourishment. And what with the pain of his joints and the anguish of having strangers tramping all over his house, and of pleading with the Mayor, and of seeing his money fetched out from its hiding-places and counted out on the table, the miserable old man was so much dazed and confused that he never thought to take down the wreath of ash and elder and the horseshoe and the key. That is why, when a week or two had gone by and no sign had shown how long this trance would continue, the Mayor and Councillors decided that as Tom, Dick and Harry could be of no further use to the town as chimney-sweeps, they might perhaps earn an honest penny for it as the "Marvels of the Age".

So the Mayor's man with a flowing white muslin band round his black hat, and his two mutes—carrying bouquets of lilies in their hands—came with his hand-cart and fetched the three bodies away. A roomy glass case had been made for them of solid Warwickshire oak, with a fine chased lock and key. And by the time that the Waits had begun to sing their carols in the snow, the three children had been installed in their glass case on the upper floor of the Cheriton Museum and lay slumbering on and on, quiet as Snowwhite in the dwarfs' coffin, the gentle daylight falling fairly on their quiet faces—though during the long summer days a dark blind was customarily drawn over the glass whenever the sun shone too fiercely at the window.

News of this wonder spread fast, and by the following Spring visitors from all over the world—even from cities as remote as Guanojuato and Seringapatam—came flocking into Warwickshire merely to gaze a while at the sleeping Chimney-Sweeps: at 6d. a time. After which a fair proportion of them went on to Stratford to view the church where lie William Shakespeare's honoured bones. Indeed Mrs. Giles, the old woman who set up an apple and ginger-bread stall beside the Museum, in a few years made so much money out of her wares that she was able to bring up her nine orphaned grandchildren all but in comfort, and to retire at last at the age of sixty to a four-roomed cottage not a hundred yards from that of Anne Hathaway's herself.

In course of time the Lord-Lieutenant and the Sheriffs and the Justices of the Peace and the Bishop and the mayors of the neighbouring towns, jealous no doubt of this fame and miracle in their midst, did their utmost to persuade and compel the Mayor and Corporation of Cheriton to remove the Boys to the county-town—the Earl himself promising to lodge them in an old house not a stone's-throw distant from the lovely shrine of his ancestors, Beauchamp Chapel. But all in vain. The people of Cheriton held tight to their rights: and the Lord Chief Justice after soberly hearing both sides at full length wagged his wigged head in their favour.

For fifty-three years the Sleeping Boys slept on. During this period the Town Council had received One Hundred and Twenty Three Thousand, Five Hundred and Fifty-Five sixpences in fees alone (i.e. £3,088 17s. 6d.). And nearly every penny of this vast sum was almost clear profit. They spent it wisely too—widened their narrow chimneys, planted lime-trees in the High Street and ash and willow beside the river, built a foun ain and a large stone dove-cot, and set apart a wooded meadowland with every comfort wild creatures can hope to have bestowed on them by their task-master, Man.

Then, one fine day, the curator—the caretaker—of the Museum, who for forty years had never once missed dusting the 'prentices glass case first thing in the morning, fell ill and had to take to his bed. And his niece, a pretty young thing, nimble and high-spirited, came as his deputy for a while, looked after the Museum, sold the tickets, and kept an eye on the visitors in his stead. She was only seventeen; and was the very first person who had ever been heard to sing in the Museum—though of course it was only singing with her lips all but closed, and never during show-hours.

And it was Summer-time, or rather the very first of May. And as each morning she opened the great door of the Museum and ascended the wide carved staircase and drew up the blinds of the tall windows on the upper floor, and then turned—as she always turned—to gaze at the Three Sleepers (and not even a brass farthing to pay), she would utter a deep sigh as if out of the midst of a happy dream.

"You lovely things!" she would whisper to herself. "You lovely, lovely things!" She had a motherly heart; and the wisps of her hair were as transparent as the E-string of a fiddle in the morning light. And the glance of her blue eyes rested on the glass case with such compassion and tenderness that if mere looking could have awakened the children they would have been dancing an Irish jig with her every blessed morning.

Being young, too, she was inclined to be careless, and had even at times broken off a tiny horn of coral, or a half-hidden scale from the mermaid's tail for a souvenir of Cheriton to any young stranger that particularly took her fancy. Moreover, she had never been

told anything about the magicry of keys or horseshoes or iron or ash or elder, having been brought up at a School where wizardry and witchcraft were never so much as mentioned during school hours. How could she realize then that the little key of the glass case and the great key of the Museum door (which, after opening both, she had dropped out of her pocket by accident plump into the garden well) could keep anybody or anything out, or in, even when the doors were wide open?

That very morning there had been such a pomp of sunshine in the sky, and the thrushes were singing so shrilly in the new-leafed lime trees as she came along to her work, that she could resist her pity and yearning no longer. Having drawn up the blinds on the upper floor, in the silence she gently raised the three glass lids of the great glass case and propped them back fully open. And one by one—after first listening at their lips as stealthily as if in hope of hearing what their small talk might be in their dreams—she kissed the slumbering creatures on their stone-cold mouths. And as she kissed Harry she fancied she heard a step upon the stair. And she ran out at once to see.

No one. Instead, as she stood on the wide staircase listening, her young face tilted and intent, there came a waft up it as of spiced breezes from the open spaces of Damascus. Not a sound, no more than a breath, faint and yet almost unendurably sweet of Spring—straight across from the bird-haunted, sheep-grazed meadows skirting the winding river: the perfume of a whisper. It was as if a distant memory had taken presence and swept in delight across her eyes. Then stillness again, broken by the sounding as of a voice smaller than the horn of a gnat. And then a terrible sharp crash of glass. And out pell-mell came rushing our three young friends, the chimney-sweeps, their dream-shapes home at last.

Now Old Nollykins by this time had long been laid in his grave. So even if anyone had been able to catch them, Tom, Dick and Harry would have swept no more chimneys for him. Nor could even the new Mayor manage it. Nor the complete Town Council. Nor the Town Crier, though he cried twice a day to the end of the year: "O-yèss! O-yèss!! O-yèss!!! Lost, stolen, or strayed: The Three World-Famous and Notorious Sleeping Boys of Warwickshire." Nor even the Lord Lieutenant. Nor even the mighty Earl.

As for the mound by the pollard willows—well, what clever Wide-awake would ever be able to give any news of that?